The Rising Sap

Other Books by F. W. Thomas:

Extra Turns (1917)
Saturday Nights (1923)
Low and I: A Cooked Tour in London (1923)
Merry Go Round (1924)
Rain and Shine (1924)
Cobbler's Wax (1925)
The Low and I Holiday Book (1925)
Week-Ends (1925)
All A-Blowing (1927)
Windfalls (1932)
The Merrygo Almanack (1933)
The Ballads of Barnacle Bill and Other Jingles (1943)
The Story of Searchlight (1954)
Tales From Stonecutter Street (2010)
Star Turns (2011)

The Rising Sap

F. W. Thomas

Edited by Richard Simms

Richard Simms Publications

This paperback first edition published in 2013

Richard Simms Publications, Surrey, England

ISBN: 978-0-9556942-8-8

The articles and sketches in this collection were originally published in *The Star* newspaper throughout 1914.

With special thanks to Morgan Wallace, Robin Andrews, David Andrews and Wendy Marriott.

For more information please visit the F. W. Thomas web page:

http://thestarfictionindex.atwebpages.com/f_w.htm

Contents

Introduction

In my previous selection of F. W. Thomas' sketches for the London evening newspaper *The Star*, I assembled the best of those that were published in the paper from 1912 to 1913. While offering what I thought were some fine examples of his early writing style, I felt that *Star Turns* surely deserved a sequel. Not least because by 1914, Thomas' star (forgive the pun) was very much in the ascendant; the author maintaining his upward momentum with a marvellous series of humorous yarns that just seemed to get better and better.

And so to this collection.

Now raising a young family at his home in Chiswick, by 1914 Thomas was well settled at the paper's bustling offices in Bouverie St, situated just off Fleet Street. Under the mentoring of his editor Ernest Parke, a stream of inspired tales flowed from the pen of Thomas in the opening months of this year. Appearing in *The Star* every Saturday, these highly readable yet quirky stories provided an amusing diversion from everyday life to thousand of Londoners sat on trains, trams and omnibuses on the journey home from work—or comfortably ensconced by their living room fires on a Saturday evening.

Whether it was something in his pipe, or just a case of being inspired by the promise of longer days, Thomas' contributions to the paper at this time were among some of his best yet. However, by the August of 1914 and the outbreak of the Great War, the stories presented in the final half this book take on a more telling historical interest and a markedly different tone. I will discuss some of these particular sketches later on in this essay.

The opening story in this book, "The Return" was printed in *The Star* on January 3, 1914, and sees the brief reappearance of the author's bonneted housekeeper, Mrs. Boddy. Readers of *Star Turns* may recall her as rather irritating! The scene of this story is New Year's Eve, with Thomas—clearly not a fan of this time of year—determined to retire to bed well before midnight. Proving to be another of his occasional excursions into light fantasy, "The Return" sees his plans to do so interrupted by a supernatural visitation that turns out to be the ghost of his 14-year-old self. Thomas junior has a bone to pick with Thomas senior: he is none too happy at the way his older version has turned out in later life. All those ambitious dreams of youth come to naught …

This dollop of silliness is followed by "The Pedlar." The setting this time is the South Downs. A peripatetic salesman joins Thomas on one of his countryside walks. Trudging along the dusty roads, the seller of sundry portable items stops over at various Sussex villages nestling between the rolling hills and tries to tempt the inhabitants to purchase the wares he carries in his knapsack.

"The Pedlar" and the title story to this collection are typical of Thomas' rustic yarns. In the former, the author has to skilfully avoid being talked into buying anything; in "The Rising Sap," a vociferous local similarly provides unwelcome company for Thomas as he hikes his way through an area of rural splendour. In this latter story, his travelling companion is a butcher by trade. Thomas' attempts to read inspiring verse out loud from the anthology of poems he has brought with him are interrupted by the meat man's depressingly down to earth monologue about the quality of the nine pigs he is considering buying from a local farmer.

With the stage shifting back to the author's house in Chiswick, "The Collector" is a very funny anecdotal piece about how Thomas handles a home visit by a tax collector. He succeeds in verbally tying the taxman up in knots with what his increasingly flustered and confused guest eventually describes as "this infernal drivel." One can't help thinking that Thomas was letting off a bit of steam when he wrote this tale.

The golden age of the silent movie provides the historical backdrop for " 'Effects'." Thomas befriends a young lad employed by a picture house as a sound effects man. In this far away era of early cinematic history, a film showing to an audience would often be accompanied by suitable accompanying sounds to simulate what is transpiring on the screen. Thomas learns how ingenious the young fellow is; a resourceful soul capable of creating a variety of sonic imitations using whatever materials he has to hand, all to augment the audience's appreciation of whatever silent feature was showing at the time. Thus the sound of a gun shot in a western movie is supplied by slapping two pieces of wood together, and so on.

Sadly, with the coming of the "Talkies" the skills displayed by clever chaps like this would have become redundant, at least in this particular context. To my mind, there is something rather poignant about " 'Effects'," providing as it does a first-hand glimpse of a long gone phenomenon that has passed out of living memory.

There is little that is out of date or redundant about "The Stores." An exercise in humour and frustration, this story sees Thomas lost in a labyrinthine London department store in search of a present for his godson. His odyssey through various sections of this vast emporium lengthens—to the point where he ends up wondering whether he will ever make it out of the shop before he dies of old age!

"The Gypsy" takes us back to the open air and the countryside. A day off work on a fine spring day (as I have presented the stories here chronologically, readers will hopefully get a sense of the passing of the seasons as they progress through this book) finds *The Star's* resident humorist traversing the Pilgrim's Way, "that ancient road that runs from Canterbury to the West." The opening paragraphs of "The Gypsy" reveal a seasoned walker's deep appreciation for nature's beauty. Thomas remarks on the transient splendour of spring flowers peeking out of the hedgerows; the exquisite sight of bluebells and primroses "bent under the heavy dew"; the call of a cuckoo and the simple pleasure of smoking a pipe while perched on the trunk of a fallen beech. Typically, Thomas' meditations on an idyllic landscape come falling down with a thud at the appearance of an interloper, in this case a loudmouthed gypsy girl ... or so she seems at first.

Remember those comical train journeys depicted in *Star Turns*? You'll find a few here as well. Under Thomas' beady eye, such raw material is transformed into hilarious little yarns such as "The

Excursion." Pity our narrator (or just laugh) as his First Class carriage is invaded by a score of noisy children on a Sunday School outing. "Travel Talk" has a similar theme, with Thomas entertained on a train journey home from work by a pair of opinionated young girls. A few choice interjections from the experienced journalist, and the wickedly irreverent double act are moved to further scathing remarks about their elders.

By the summer of 1914, Thomas was flourishing at *The Star*, writing a string of delightful sketches that continued to be printed in the paper every Saturday. Varied in theme and content, pieces such as "Under the Tape" and "The Pathetic Pen" showcase a quicksilver mind at work. The phonetic spelling and easy flow of dialogue testify to Thomas' talent as a keen observer of the way ordinary people, from all walks of life, actually talk.

There's great dialogue to be found in "Under the Tape," which sees him in a tailor's shop in need of a new lounge suit. Here is an author clearly relating an event from his personal experience ... if slightly embellished in the interests of telling a good story! On measuring him up for a fitting, the tailor huffs and sighs, not only at the sorry state of the overworn suit Thomas is still wearing, but also at the increased waistlines he sees in all his regular customers. His client very funnily objects to this belittlement, and furthermore rebels against the tailor's insistence that he adopt a more modern dress style. Thomas would have been well into his thirties at the time this story was written, and was evidently loath to leave his comfort zone by replacing his old attire with possibly ill fitting new garments.

Such sartorial conflicts are absent from "A Pathetic Pen," although the author's companion for this story is described as being rather shabbily dressed! The scene is yet another from a disappeared time: a band playing to a seated audience in a London park one summer evening. This very civilised and genteel pastime was a common enough entertainment for the capital's population back in the Edwardian age. Reclining on a deck chair, Thomas' enjoyment of Beethoven, to the accompaniment of a glorious sunset, is interrupted by an annoyingly insistent fellow trying to sell him a gold pen. A strained conversation ensues but, as always, Thomas sees the funny side to this, and turns the incident into a sketch sprinkled with wry humour.

A fishing village situated in an idyllic bay in the West Country provides the picturesque setting of "The Arrival." It was here that Thomas returned each year to take his annual summer holiday, and in this piece we get a wonderful sense of place. There are some lovely poetic touches: the gull hanging above in the "illimitable blue"; the "magic light" that comes up out of the sea at eventide; and the "pink fingers of honeysuckle" at the side of the winding lane. The provincial dialect is also keenly observed, as well as the local names, such as Sam Trevagissey. "The Arrival" chronicles the author's dealings with various residents who explain in graphic detail the injuries they sustained in transporting Thomas' trunk down the hill to the inn at which he will be staying. A succession of tips for their troubles placates each villager in turn.

News of the outbreak of the Great War had reached the village by the time Thomas penned "Called Up." Published in *The Star* on August 15, 1914, as an aside, it's noteworthy also for the reappearance of Miriam, the innkeeper's daughter who appeared in two of the stories collected in *Star Turns*. Thomas learns from Miriam that her "young man" has been called up for military service, although it turns out that he is too young for the Territorials. Instead he is seen serving his duty on the Home Front as a scout patrolling a level crossing.

"Called Up" does not (and was never intended to) provide the reader with any profound insight into the nation's psyche at this momentous time in history. But it does give us an interesting snapshot of the impact the news of war had on a small, isolated coastal community.

Returning to the city, from hereon Thomas' contributions to the newspaper were inevitably informed by the effect of the war on the people of London. Despite maintaining his gently humorous take on events, there is a feverish, compelling intensity to some of his narratives in the latter half of 1914. Thomas was evidently inspired to produce some of the best writing of his career by the grave international situation.

The reaction of a variety of Londoners during the opening months of the war are chronicled in sketches such as "Time-Expired." This piece was written when Kitchener was staring out of posters on walls across Britain entreating young men to serve their King by joining the army: "Your Country Needs You." In "Time-Expired" an old soldier reflects the attitude of many in this period; working men caught up in Kitchener's recruitment drive, much of whom were not particularly patriotic and had little understanding of the political reasons behind the conflict breaking out in Europe in the first place. One is reminded of the words of the late Harry Patch, "The Last Tommy" who in his final years stated in an interview for the BBC that he still had no idea what he had been fighting for.

Out and about on the streets of London, overheard conversations gave Thomas the inspiration for his sketches in general. "The Decision" reads that way; a discussion between two young men seated on a park bench by the lake in St. James' Park as they decide whether or not to enlist. The scene is vivid and real, with the recruitment tents beckoning to the undecided pair in the distance. One a grocer, the other a butcher, the men witnessed by Thomas are seen considering the pros and cons of joining up.

This piece appears to us all these years later as a quite touching meditation on youthful impetuosity. Indeed, it is an unpalatable fact that a good number of volunteers signed up for duty on a whim, often down to what we now call "peer group pressure," or the simple machismo thrill of promised adventure. Moreover, it is uncomfortable today to reflect upon the likely fate of men such as those depicted in "The Decision." Basing their decision on the flip of a coin, they may well have ended up dying, along with so many thousands of others, fighting in the Battle of the Somme. At the time this story was written, Thomas, in common with his contemporaries, could not have foreseen the unimaginable carnage and huge loss of life that was to occur in the ensuing years on the battlefields of Northern Europe and further afield.

It is perhaps interesting to note that Thomas himself did not enlist for the army at this time. Involuntary conscription was not introduced until 1916, and in retrospect there is a slight question mark over the reason why Thomas was spared from the draft. It has been surmised by his grandchildren as to why this was so. By 1917, his popularity as a humorist was on the rise with the publication of the first book collection of his short stories, the best selling *Extra Turns*. Mindful of this, the authorities may well have thought that he was better off continuing to lift the spirits of Londoners—and no doubt some soldiers on active duty—with his funny sketches. Furthermore, at the time of the Great War, Thomas was newly married with two very young children; this consideration, coupled with his profession, could have been an influence on the decision to exempt him from conscription.

But getting back to the stories in this book, "The Sergeant" shows us that Thomas did undergo some basic training as a soldier. As part of a motley crew of rather unfit men of various professions—possibly intended to serve on the Home Front—Thomas is put through his paces by a gruff old veteran of various conflicts who has seen it all and is determined to make soldiers out of his charges. The clerks, hosiers, artists and plumbers (as Thomas describes his comrades) struggle to keep up!

"The Sergeant" spawned two sequels in later issues of *The Star* dating from the autumn of 1914, "Discipline" and the curiously evocative " 'Algernon'." The latter story is, in my view, one of the most powerful pieces in this collection. It sees Thomas and his compatriots at an informal gathering of their regiment, getting the low down on what is really happening in the battles played out on the muddy fields across the Channel. They proceed to hear from a wounded soldier a first-hand account of the reality of trench warfare.

We return to the ironic tone of "The Decision" with "The Adventurers," a briskly told vignette about two soldiers in training taking a break while sitting in a farmer's field. They are an odd couple, one coming from a well-to-do background, while the other is a cockney through and through. Their very different reasons for enlisting are both painfully comic and trivial. To our modern eyes, in the light of the human tragedy and subsequent "lost generation" that was to follow, this story is an exercise in black humour.

Another story I am pleased to reprint here is "The Mother," which gives us the perspective of proud and yet concerned parents at the time so many young men were marching off to war. Thomas is sharing a train carriage with a man and wife whose son is serving in Europe. Their worry over what might befall him moves the couple to reassure one another that he will be coming home. In his quirky way, the author relates this conversation with a skilful eye for detail.

One final story I would like to give mention to is "The Atrocity." There was an influx of Belgian refugees to London in the early months of the war. Taking advantage of this phenomenon, a young girl who has been genuinely hurt in an accident involving a bicycle poses as a Belgian refugee in a London street—with passers by making the intended assumption and offering sympathy and the charity of a shilling or two. In Thomas' work during this period, his trademark humour was mixed in with real life happenings until the two were inseparable. The black humour on display here represents an honest observer at work; a wry reflection on the inappropriate reactions some members of the British public had to what was a serious subject at the time.

I have highlighted in this introductory essay just some of the stories included in this volume. There are other gems to be found within the pages of this book that I will leave readers to discover for themselves. These sketches, intended for the most part as light entertainment all those years ago, provide a unique perspective into a period of British history that still intrigues many people today.

Republished for the first time since their original appearance in a London evening newspaper nearly a century ago, in this book are the writings of a journalist and humorist whose career was on an upward trajectory. That his stories in this period coincide with the death throes of the Edwardian age and the coming of the Great War (that was to change Britain forever) makes them particularly fascinating.

So let F. W. Thomas cast his journalistic eye over these events and allow us to travel back to this long gone era through his gifts for humour, wonderful dialogue and social commentary. He was writing for a newspaper, not for the ages. I submit that the stories assembled here are all the more real because of that. Enjoy.

Richard Simms
Surrey, England
December, 2012

The Return

At the midnight of the year it is good, the copybooks tell us, to spend a little time in quiet meditation; taking a mental survey of the past twelve months, auditing one's books, and striking a balance, the profit and loss in pounds sterling and avoirdupois. That is the theory of it.

Actual practice differs somewhat from this. The man next door but one, for instance. He once paid a visit to Scotland, and every year since he drags his family into the garden, rain or shine, and as the iron tongue of midnight tolls twelve, bawls "Auld Lang Syne" into the atmosphere with an Aldgate Pump accent.

These ceremonies seem superfluous. The occasion is melancholy enough in itself, without, as it were, rubbing it in. We are a year older, a year nearer becoming adipocere in Kensal Green; and what shall it profit a man to meditate upon the errors and omissions of the dead past, or to make rococo noises in the back garden, waking all the dogs for miles round?

Therefore the wise man shuts his eyes to the calendar, and goes to bed before the syrens and bells get in their deadly work. There is only one 8.15 in the morning, and it doesn't wait.

It was with this object in view that on Wednesday night last I dragged the big chair to the fender at nine o'clock, and surrounded myself with cushions, a tumbler, and a piece of lemon. Bed at 10.30, I said. Then in came Mrs. Boddy, trembling a little as to the bonnet.

"Please, I've busted the 'ead off the duchess on the mantelpiece, and there's a young gentleman to see you."

"You will find the fish glue where you left it last time," I said; "and who is the young gentleman?"

17

" 'E didn't give no name," said Mrs. Boddy. "A nice young gentleman. Asked for you. Down at the mat. Says it's important an' private." She went to show him up.

"And what is the trouble?" I asked. He looked serious.

"You've got fat," he said suddenly.

This was rude, and I told him so. "Who the dickens are you?" I asked.

"I'm you," he said, and looked ever so sad. Somehow his face seemed familiar, and there was some ink on his collar that I thought I recognised.

"Well, well," I said; "these things must be. I suppose you are going to trot out a lot of cheap platitudes about the flight of time. But you're nearly three hours too early, you know. Midnight's the hour, when churchyards yawn and all that sort of thing. You'll have the Spooks' Union after you for time cribbing or speeding up. However, get on with your moralising."

"I'm not exactly a ghost, and I'm not going to moralise," said the boy. "I'm you, at fourteen, and I've come to know how I—how you are getting on. How am I?"

"Not too dusty, although on this particular evening it is my usual custom to retire well before midnight," I replied.

"I'm disappointed," he said. "I thought better things of you after all my plans. Thirty something, aren't you? And sitting beside a roaring fire, stuffing hot drinks. Looks as if you'd made a proper mess of things. You're fat, too, and you go over at the shoulders."

"Confound it all!" I said. "What d'you want? What's the matter with me? If you don't like it, you know the way you came in."

"No sense in getting stuffy about it," he said. "You see, I've got an interest in you. Sort of shareholder; and I'm a bit cut up now I've seen you. After all my fine plans, I was reckoning on you being somebody; something decent, you know, and out of the ordinary. And now look at you! An explorer, I thought; 'stead of which—"

"Oh, yes!" I answered pettishly. "The dreams of youth are long, long dreams; but, as you remark, they don't come off. A year before that it was an engine driver, and before that a van boy, and a pirate, and a Red Indian. You can't have it all ways, you know. There's no demand for explorers these days. One takes a bus, and I—well, I'm satisfied, more or less."

"That's the sort of thing I expected you to say," said Me; "but all the same it's a lie. You're not satisfied. You're just bluffing." He stared into the fire for a little; then looked me up and down again.

"What do you do?" he asked. I waved my hand towards the desk.

"No, not that tosh!" he said. "I mean, what do you *do*? Games. Keep up your footer and cricket? I used to be a dab at games, you remember. What's your batting average?"

"I'm afraid I haven't one," I answered. "Too busy, you know; and besides, one must give up games sooner or later. Life is not all footer."

"I never thought you'd be a funk," said Me. "That's what it is. Funk! And I reckoned you were going to play for your county. S'pose it's bellows-to-mend with you, smoking those rifle-range cigars. And you were—I was the fastest of my year up to the 200 yards. Do anything in that line?"

"Only in the mornings," I said. "I'm not in training, you know. One must live."

"No games at all?" asked Me reproachfully.

"Only cribbage and patience, and things like that," I said; "and I play rather a decent game of croquet."

"Croquet, oh crumbs!" said Me. "Ever try marbles?" He walked across the room to the bookshelves.

"They look a stuffy old lot," he said presently. "Where's my 'Coral Island' and the 'Buffalo Runners,' and all those? And my silkworms?"

"I swapped the lot for an inner tube years ago," I answered. "Snorky Proggins had 'em. Remember Snorky? That's his photo over there."

"Crikey!" said Me. "Is that old Snorkey? Weird sort of cove, wasn't he? Always messing about with batteries and things. He was going to be an inventor, I remember. Looks like a barber's assistant."

"Actually," I said, "Mr. Horace Proggins is the manager of the Kilburn branch of the Bank of Mesopotamia, and doing very well."

"That's better than you, anyway," snorted Me. "I never thought you'd be a jolly old ink-slinger, swotting over books and things all day. If you only knew—but I s'pose it's no good talking. At least, I reckoned you were going to keep yourself fit, but you look all soft and flabby—" (I bowed.) "—and you want a hair cut, and—and—well really, you look an awful wreck, you know. Your chest has slipped down, and—and you dress like a—like a—I don't know." His eyes travelled slowly from my head to my heels.

"I s'pose it's too late for you to do anything really fine now," he said. "You're old. A straight man with decent shoulders, an out-of-doors man, I'd reckoned on. A man who'd done something. And here you are, in a stuffy old room that stinks of tobacco, catching the same old train every morning—" ("Not the same train every morning," I said.) "—and wearing a bowler hat." He sighed heavily.

"You've mucked it; that's what you've done. Mucked it. I'm sorry."

"Yes," I said, "by those standards, I suppose, we've mucked it between us. Most people do. But—but—" and I tried to think of some excuses.

A coal fell with a rattle into the fender. Mucked it ... Oh, yes! Of course. I remember! Saucy young pup.

From the garden below there came the noise of a man who proclaimed to all who listened, his intention of drinking a right gude-willy waught, for the sake of Auld Lang Syne; and the fire being out, I crept into my bed.

The Pedlar

From the five pines that top the Beacon to the crown of the next hill but one was six miles; and over that crest I should find the "Three Kings" and tobacco. Therefore I forgot the blister on my heel, and thought only of the great cloud of smoke that I would presently blow to heaven; and so strode on.

On and up the hill; past the patch of bare earth where no grass will grow (there it was that Pett the Miller slew the great dog Toth after a fight lasting four days); past the Frozen Man of Ketling; through Abel's orchard, where the apple trees bear nothing but mistletoe; and so to the valley of Ob.

Now this last is in two parts, which are two hollows scooped out by Ob with his scoop, a big thing like a bank clerk's shovel.

If ever you see Ob, you run. For he is bigger than a cathedral, and his shape is the shape of the County of Cheshire; and he eats coke and Sussex villages, with their parish halls and glebe lands, their Carnegie libraries and skittle alleys, parsons, squarsons, and panel doctors; all the lot he eats, scooping them up with his scoop—so! Hence the South Downs.

And in the creases under his eyes, and in the folds of his dewlaps, lie tons and tons of cinders which make him sneeze; and when Ob sneezes, down on the coast they hoist the North Cone, and Lloyd's Agent sharpens his pencil.

Into this valley I went, digging my heels in, for it was 1 in 20 and slippery with frost. Up the further slope, not slackening my pace one bit, for the tobacco on the other side.

And then there was none. No tobacco and no "Three Kings." All was clear grass from the top of the hill to the bottom. Not a house or a haystack or a hencoop. Said I, "Ob has been at it again," and crossed my fingers and touched wood.

But I must have lost my way; these hills are so like one another. Perhaps over the next ridge— So we started again, my empty pouch and I, striking off to the right, where I saw a telegraph pole, and so to a white and winding road that promised succour. For roads mean inns, and since the "Three Kings" was lost to me, why then, I would be content with the "Sailor's Return" or the "Winking Panther."

Summer time, with that white road searing the eyes, would have seen me annoyed; but the frost and the bright sun worked otherwise, and I sang. For that helps one to hurry.

Steaming cows looked over the gates with big, sad eyes; crows flapped lazily upwards at my song; and there was no man in all that world but me. Not even a wisp of smoke from a chimney pot.

Under big trees the road went, and last year's brown leaves still hung on the briers, all gemmed with hoar frost. I picked one up, and saw growing on it a tiny forest of fairy trees, with branches and twigs, all wrought out of diamonds by the frost. I breathed on the forest and it melted away.

Then I wanted a smoke, and started off once more with great strides that seemed to make no difference whatever to the length of that long white road. A bend, a new view, and a man in it.

There he was, a mile ahead, and his legs looked longer than mine. I ran. But suppose he did not smoke!

Of course he would smoke. The gods would not play a joke like that. I ran faster, lest he should smoke it all before I got there.

He did not smoke. He was a lifelong non-smoker and total abstainer; and all the little hills laughed like anything. But he had a nice face, and I refrained from killing him. Besides, he was six-feet-two, and his voice was like the deep trembly notes of an organ. On his back was a leather knapsack, in his hand a great staff shod with iron, and the soles of his boots were an inch thick.

"I am walking," he said, "to Marlpit-under-the-Hill, where I hope to do good business.

"Spring is on the road, laggard spring; and I have here"—he swung the knapsack round to his chest—"a certain and wonderful cure for coughs, colds, pains in the back, catarrh, rheumatism, and sciatica."

"Lumbago, spots on the face, toothache, and cataract," said I.

"Mumps, whooping cough, croup, and German measles," said he.

"Ingrowing toenails, loss of appetite after meals, and poor man's gout," said I.

"Thank you," said he. "I hadn't thought of those."

"Is Marlpit-under-the-Hill so unhealthy?" I asked.

"For the robust," he answered. "I have hymn-books, ancient and modern, shaving soap, goldbeater's skin, dictionaries, all the latest copyright songs, words and music, rubber heels, court plaister, and books of riddles."

We walked along for a space saying nothing; I sucking at my empty pipe, he droning like a bee over a clover clump.

"A brave day," he said presently. "See how the sun sprinkles the fields with precious jewels, pure crystals to take the place of summer's more gaudy gems. On such a day— Look here, if you haven't got anything the matter with you, can I book an order for the Hundred Best Books?" I thought not.

"Or the Hundred Best Pictures?" I was sure he could not. Nor for the Arabian Nights adapted for the young, nor for the Family Physician, the Lives of the Saints, or America's Aristocracy in fortnightly parts.

He was a persevering pedlar. During two quick miles he tried to insure my life, sell me a sparking plug, some double-width calico for pillow cases, and an electric torch.

"Is there nothing in this world you want? Is there nothing the matter with you?" he asked. "Are you sure you have not lurking within you—?"

"Quite sure!" I said. "I have a blister on my heel, but that is all."

"A needle," he said, and swung his pack round again. "A needle, and a piece of worsted. Push needle through blister, draw worsted after it—one penny."

"I'll wait until I get home," I said. "But a smoke would lighten the burden of my blister."

"I should have thought of it before," he answered, and took off his hat. "I have here a mixture of herbs, flowers of the field; really a magic cure for asthma and tight breathing. But I understand it goes very well in a pipe. Threepence."

Ahead I saw a pole by the roadside, and a board that swung at the top of the pole, and on the board a capering white horse. I took to my heels, and left the pedlar talking sewing machines.

The Piper

You know the sort of noise a circular saw makes; a circular saw, that is, mingled with a dash of unripe rhubarb, and a touch of Dying Pig ("All made to fall down an' die one penny"). There was a noise like that outside our Town Hall last night, with a crowd of youngsters standing round and watching it.

In the middle of the noise, right at its heart, was a gorgeous man. As a matter of fact, he was making the noise himself, blowing it out of an armful of tubes and ribbons that sprouted from his chest. And as he walked the noise enveloped him like a cloud, so that he travelled in a haze of circular saws and Dying Pigs.

Not such a haze but that he shone through it. He would have shone through a brick wall. He was resplendent; six feet of him, glittering from head to heel with belts and buckles, medals and sporrans, dirks and daggers. He was more than a mere man; he was a procession.

With feet turned well out at an angle of 45, he walked quickly up and down, side stepping over the puddles, and swaying rhythmically from the hips. And all the while he blew his monstrous noise into the air. That was what he was there for, and he did it well, with cheeks distended to splitting point.

Unlike the melancholy and mercenary folk who jerk out "Even me," or "Yes, there's room," he cast no longing eyes up at the windows as he passed; but looking fixedly at the ground, intent on his work and the puddles, he just blew and blew and blew.

Some Highland chieftain, I thought, happened on evil days; driven from his ancestral deer forest by a voracious ground landlord or marauding cateran. I would talk with him when he had done insulting our Town Hall with his half-civilised cacophony.

Nay, I would do more. I would address him in his own tongue. Perchance the sound of his "native wood notes wild" might bring joy and comfort to this magnificent piper, who piped in an alien land, where none danced.

Not that I am Scots; but I have seen Harry Lauder once or twice, read a great deal of the kail-yard school of literature, and yelled welcome to the New Year at the top of Ludgate Hill.

There was a sound like red-hot barbed wire, and with a squelch of anguish the Dying Pig breathed his last. A horrible death.

A penny crashed to the pavement, and the Highlander, wrapping his plaid around him, strode off into the shadows, I after him. Now for Crockett and Maclaren.

"It's a braw nicht the nicht, is it no?" I asked.

"Hooch ay!" he answered as he turned to look at me.

" 'Tis a pleasure to meet one who shall skirl sae blithely at the pibroch," I ventured.

"Hooch ay!" said the Scot. (We're getting along famously, thought I.)

"Ilka time ye skirl," said I, "ye 'mind me of depairted joys, an' all that sort of thing, ye ken."

"Hooch ay!" said he.

"An' wit way will ye no' gies a skirl the noo?" I asked. (You'll find that in "Wee Macgregor.")

"Hooch ay!" said the Scot.

"I'se uphand ye're acquent wi' the Lament for Donal' the De'il," I suggested, and said it twice, I was so proud of it.

"Hooch ay!" said the Scot. Not a conversationalist, evidently. Or was he pulling my leg? I would try him.

"And do you know—I beg your pardon—div ye ken the noo the Wail for the Red Sons of Tosh?" I said.

"Hooch ay!" he answered.

"Or the lament for Weelum Bailey, with his maist joyfu' return?" said I.

"Hooch ay!" said he.

"Erin go bragh!" said I.

"Hooch ay!" said he.

"Bleak blows the blast across the braes o' Balquhidder," said I.

"Hooch ay!" said he.

"Hier spricht man Deutsch," said I.

"Hooch ay!" said he.

"Ici on parle français," said I.

"Now you've been an' gone an' done it," said he. "I've seen that on the winders at the tailor's shop. Might 'ave knowed you was 'avin' me on a bit o' string. What's the game, guv'nor?"

"And did you understand a word of what I was saying?" I asked.

"Not a word," he said. "But I guessed you was a Jock, 'cos I've 'eard somethink like it before on the 'Alls. So I trots out my 'ooks an' eyes, till you give the game away with that there Italian stuff."

"Then you're a whited sepulchre," I said.

"Hooch ay!" said he. "But I thought there was money in it. That's all the Scotch I know. 'Hooch ay' is. An' I learnt it off the bloke what sold me this rig out, down in 'Oundsditch. Dossy duds, ain't they?"

"And so it doesn't pay?" I asked.

"Pay? Not it! I wore out two pair o' boots last week, an' made about eighteenpence a day. Don't do to stand still, you know. 'Tain't playin' the game. I s'pose the bloke what invented this 'ere thing used to walk up an' down to try an' get away from 'isself.

"Don't 'alf give you a 'eadache neither. Well, thank 'eaven tomorrow's Sunday, an' I'm off duty ... I should think the bloke what invented these things was the same bloke what invented Scotch whisky. Sort of an afterthought. One'd drive you to the other. Wouldn't matter which you started on.

"An' cold! Tomorrow I'm goin' to put on two pairs of trousis, out of spite."

"But where did you learn to play the bagpipes?" I asked. "In Houndsditch also?"

"Play? I wasn't playin' 'em," he said. "Not really! Did it sound as rotten as that? I just blew the bag full of wind and let it oozle out of the toobs, an' wobbled me fingers over the 'oles. An' there you are!

"Tell you what though, guv'nor. If you'll learn me some of that Scotch you was firin' at me, I'll let you off buyin' me a drink. 'Ow do we go?"

"Ye maunderin' killiethumpie," I said. "Div ye thenk I'll be seen stravagin' but an' ben the toon wi' sic an' awfu' fule as yersel?" And a lot more nearly as good, and about as intelligible.

"Not 'alf!" said the piper. "I mean, 'Hooch ay!' "

The Rising Sap

Mr. Pettigrew and his green barrow with one wheel have sprinkled bone meal all over the grass; and "Don't you dare set foot on that there lawn for a full fortnight," he said. The way he talks, you'd think I owed him money.

Earlier in the week a timid snowdrop shoved a big pebble aside, and climbed up through the mould to see how things looked.

Signs of the times, these. And yet it is difficult to imagine, as you pile on more coal, that in a matter of months you will be seeking the shady side of the street, fanning yourself with your hat, pining for bubbly drinks with tinkling ice, and asking your friends if they can keep themselves warm; that presently there will be a heat wave in the papers with a full list of all the previous heat waves. Yet I can assure you that it will be so.

Can you not hear the headlines? The City of Dreadful Day: What Mr. Negretti Thinks. And four days later; Hotter Still: What Mr. Zambra Thinks. (Now let us all solemnly touch wood.)

Yesterday morning, feeling sadly in need of exercise, I put a book in my pocket and went to a railway station and bought three pennyworth. Waiting until the porter had finished his spring song, something about "Mary Ann, the 'Addick Smoker's Daughter," I asked him, "Does this train go to Much Partington?"

Sang he:

I listened with joy,
As I did when er boy,
To the sound of them old village bells.

"Much Partington?" I said again.

"The logs were burnin' brightly—yes, all right for Much Partington—'Twas the night when they banish all sin. Right be'ind, 'Erry! An' the bells was ringin' the Old Year out—'Urry up, there, please. Mind steppin' on!—an' the Noo—Year—in!"

A mad world, my masters; but then the temperature was something silly for February—the sun was hot through the glass roof, the sky was June's high blue, and there was a drunken gnat dancing over the platform.

They turned me out at a wooden packing case labelled "Much Partington, This Side Up"; and I found a road that led somewhere, a road of stiff clay, with big blue puddles.

Not far from the station a man was painting something on a tarred shed. I watched him for some time to see if he would do something that I knew he would do, and he did it. He painted the word TEAS, and he put the S wrong way round, as they always do. Another sign of the times.

When I pointed out his error he was rude, so I wished him well and walked on, swinging my stick. Despite the absurd warmth of the sun and the little flecks of golden swansdown in the west, the countryside was dead as any nail.

The hedges flanking the road were but a shrivelled tangle of lifeless briers, with here and there a wren playing his little whistle, or a long-shanked robin hopping ahead and cocking his wily old eye at me. Elm and oak and ash were fast asleep still, and a sparrow summed up the position, sitting on a dead branch.

"You can go on playing the giddy goat," he said to the sun, "but you don't kid me. I know it's going to rain like billy-o presently, and freeze, and thaw, and blow; and I'm not out building today, thanks all the same." Saying which he scooped up a venturesome ant and two venturesome green flies, and went his way.

Then it was I saw a figure ahead; a portly figure, well nourished and fat, that pranced over the puddles like a March lamb.

I said it was a fine day, and he said it was great. He added that he didn't know when he'd seen such a day, and I said neither did I. Then he said for Feb. it was wonderful, and I agreed that Feb. would be sorry for it later on, and repent in sackcloth and snowstorms.

We talked like that for a long time, until we seemed to have known each other for years.

"Quite a treat to get out of the hubbub on a day like this, isn't it?" I said.

He said it was, adding, "I am a butcher, you know." I did not know, but I asked him wherefore he did not butch this day; why he had thrown down the marrow bones and cleavers to come thus

Away, away, from men and towns,
To the wild wood and the downs,
To the silent wilderness.

Was it the spring time, the only pretty ring time?

No, he didn't think it was. As a matter of fact, he'd come down about some pigs, and did I know Tyecott's Farm?

"I do not," I said, "but I have here a pleasant little poem by Mr. Shelley, called 'Invitation.' I will read it to you. 'Best and brightest, come away—' "

"Tracts!" he said. "No, thanks! Pigs is what I'm after. You see, this mild weather, pork's so uncertain, and they're so cheap that I want to see 'em."

"But does not the arrival of the vernal equinox move your thoughts from pork?" I asked. "Do you not realise that below this dank ditch are bright flowers just waking? That the buds on the trees are stirring in their sticky shells? That in a thousand homes about us busy housewives are mixing gallons of brimstone and treacle in gallipots?"

He thought a little while, then answered me:

"No doubt there's a lot of truth in what you say, but you see, with pigs you've got to go so wary. 'Taint only shape and size. It's form that counts. Form. They may be heavy, but what's the good of that if half of it's got to be cut away? Fat ain't meat, is it?"

"True!" said I. "But listen to this:

Where the melting hoar frost wets

The daisy-star that never sets,
And wind-flowers and violets—"

"What makes me anxious is they're so cheap," he went on. "Either old Tyecott's hard pushed, or else there's something wrong with 'em. I wonder! You see, this mild weather plays the devil with pork. And nine's a lot. It'd be different if I cured myself, but I don't, and nine's a tidy handful to get rid of fresh, isn't it?

"He's a bit of a twister, is old Tyecott, and I had my suspicions when he wrote and asked me to come and see 'em. What would you think if a man offered you nine pigs at seven-fifteen? Wouldn't you think there was something the matter with 'em? And pork's fetching good prices nowadays, you know. There's something wrong somewhere, I'll swear. You see, with pork, this mild weather—"

Here I gave him up. Tyecott's Farm, I said, lay over there to the right, I thought.

I hope it did, and then again, for the pigs' sake, I hope it did not. But all the rest of that day I could hear the whetting of knives, and screaming. Nor did my book comfort me, for turning the leaves at random I found Whitman:

I think I could turn and live with animals,
They are so placid and self-contained …
They do not lie awake in the dark and weep for their sins.

And when the sunset came it was just the colour of apple sauce.

The Collector

I had a really splendid day yesterday. I was rude to a tax collector. I made him so wild. I shouldn't think he would try to collect a tax from me again for years. A splendid day. Don't you wish you were me?

I was asleep when he called, and that helped a lot. You see, after lunch I sat down to have a good think; but halfway through a good thought I dropped off, until his knock awakened me. One of those knocks that sound so important.

"I have called," he said, "for the Income Tax and the Inhabited House Duty. Two pounds four."

"Oh—ah—yes, of course," I said. "Two pounds four. Come inside, will you? Income Tax, I think you said. Sit down, please. And House Duty. Two (nothing in that pocket) pounds (nor there) four (no luck).

"A lot of money that, you know," I pursued. "Two pounds four. Why, it's—let's see—yes, it's nearly two pounds five, isn't it? Very nearly three pounds. Take a chair, will you? Oh—ah! Yes, of course. Well, take another."

He put his hat on the floor beside him and looked very stern. Things began to look serious. I pleaded with him. I reminded him that doubtless he had once had a mother; that obviously we had been boys together, even if in different parts of the country.

"You wouldn't be so cruel as to distrain," I said. "You couldn't. It would be too horrible. Think of my home, my reputation, my neighbours; think of anything you like; think of a number."

"I am thinking of two pounds four," said the tax collector.

"Double it," said I.

"Four pounds eight," said he.

"Take away the number you first thought of," said I.

"Two pounds four," said he.

"You must have gone wrong somewhere," I said. "When I was a boy at school the answer was always thirty-two. I really don't think you ought to be a tax collector at all.

"And now I come to think of it," I continued, "you look less and less like any tax collector I have ever known. There is a kindly fire, a much too benevolent gleam in your eye—no, the other eye. And your arithmetic is frightful."

"I can assure you that I really am the tax collector," he said, "and moreover, I am getting angry. Wasting my time here. I want two pounds four."

"Don't, please don't keep harping on that," I protested. "Two pounds four, two pounds four, all day long. That sort of thing kills all good feeling, you know. We were getting along very well until you raked that up. Think of what the Psalmist said about the love of money."

"It wasn't the Psalmist," he retorted. "Timothy said that; and I want two pounds four, or—"

"There you go again," I said. "Why not forget it for a time? Have a cigarette, and do try to lift your mind above the sordid money-grubbing of this world. Let us be friends." And I held out my hand.

He looked in it, and found it empty. "I am afraid I can't lift my mind above the two pounds four mark," he said. "I only want your word that you can't pay, and my people will do the rest."

"Meaning distraint," I said. "You would send a boozed bailiff round here to be boarded and lodged at my expense until such time as your auctioneer and estate agent found something in the house worth two pounds four? You would do that?"

"I would," said the heartless creature.

"Two pounds four," he went on. "One pound fifteen income tax on house rent under Schedule A, and nine shillings Inhabited House Duty. Total, two pounds four."

"Do you know Poe's 'Raven'?" I asked him. "Because somehow you remind me of it. 'Take thy bill from out my heart, and take thy hat from off my floor. Quoth the raven, two pounds four.' See what I mean?

"You're obsessed with those figures. You've no originality. And the nine shillings is obviously wrong. This isn't an inhabited house." He began to look nervous. "The people have gone out for the day," I said. "I'm only the plumber or the gas fitter, I forget which for the moment. Ah, yes! The gas fitter, of course. I've come to measure the gas for a new pipe. Have a cigarette?"

"You are Mr. Prendergast, are you not?" asked the collector. I smote my forehead.

"Discovered!" I cried. "At least, the name seems familiar to me. Perhaps I am. But I haven't a card on me at the moment. Prendergast, Prendergast? I know I've heard it somewhere."

"Then I must ask you not to waste any more of my time," he said. "This amount—" I walked up and down the room.

"If you say those figures once more," I said, "you leave this house forever.

"You come in here, you sit in my chair, you smoke my cigarettes, you put your hat on my floor (he picked it up), and your feet on my carpet (he picked them up, too), and you try to bully me into paying absurd sums of money that I know nothing about. You, who cannot think of the number you first thought of without getting the answer wrong. It's preposterous, it's monstrous."

"It's two pounds four," said the tax collector.

"But, my dear man," I protested, "I've got no money. Those are tram tickets that you can hear jingling; used ones. And there's nothing in the house to sell."

The collector rose. "I'm sorry, Mr. Prendergast," he said, "but I've been here—"

"Wait a minute," I interjected. "Wait half a minute. Let me think. There's something wrong. Something— Ah, I know! I was sure there was a mistake somewhere, and now I've found it. You see, my name's not Prendergast, and never was, to my knowledge. *Now* where's your two pounds four?"

"Not—not Prendergast?" stammered the collector. "This is What's-his-name Road, isn't it?"

"It is," I said sternly.

"And this is No. 5, isn't it?" he asked.

"I told you your arithmetic was rotten," I answered. "This is not No. 5."

"But on your door—the figures—" he gasped. (Have *you* ever made a tax collector gasp?)

"Yes, I know," said I. "You see this is really No. 15, but the 1 has been stolen. I think it was the man at No. 11. I know he's got a screwdriver and—of course, he wants the 1 more than I do. Twice as much." The tax collector rose, purple.

"You're a fool, sir; that's what you are," he spluttered. "Wasting my time with your infernal drivel. Twenty minutes I've been here, sir. You shall hear further about this. Impudence. Is this the way out?"

"Unless you try the window," I said. "But don't let us part in anger. Let not the sun go down— See what I mean? Perhaps now you're here, you'd like to look over the rest of the house. Or the garden. Come into the garden, tax collector, and see my daffodil taking the winds of March with beauty."

"Pah!" said the collector. "Pah!" and tore down the door, and tore down the road, and tore round the corner.

I think the man at No. 5 ought to be grateful to me.

"Effects"

The fourteen-stone villain fell from the roof of the fourteen-storey mansion without a sound; dropped like a bullet and landed like a feather. Next a cowboy with doormats round his legs polished off one or two minor villains with a noiseless revolver, and "End of Part II." appeared on the screen.

There was a devastating train smash in Part III., and a deathbed confession: four lines, which they gave us ten minutes to read; and the knots in the plot began to untie themselves, ready for the tying of the final knot.

From the shadows all round me, shadows punctuated by glowing cigarettes, came low-voiced comment, giggles and laughter, with heavy breathing at the many crises. Something just discernible beside me gave vent to a snort of disgust.

"Jever see such a rotten show?" it asked. I protested that as such shows went, this one was not at all bad. Some of it, in fact, was quite good.

"Ah," said the voice, "you mean the pictures. They're all right, if you like. Fine. Wish I 'ad 'em to work. But they're worked rotten. Now when I was 'ere, I used to make 'em sit up properly. But this chap—!"

The lights went up, and I saw the complainant, a lank youth of about twenty.

"I'm fed up," he said. "Makes me wild, the good stuff going to waste. Wish I'd got 'em. If ever you want to see pictures worked, *really* worked, you come along to my show, down at the Pink Palace. We'll show you!"

"I'm fed up, too," I said. "Let's come out together, and if you like, I'll come along to the Pink Palace with you." So we left the rotten show.

"Ah, there's nothing much doin' there this week," said the young man. "Quiet lot; Panama Canal and comics and drawin' rooms. Nothing in my line, so I'm takin' an evenin' off.

"I used to be at that show we've just come out of, before I went to the Pink Palace, and my present boss, 'e come there one night and saw my show, and 'e took me on."

"Then it's just a question of turning the handle properly," I suggested. "You object to your successor in the operating-box."

" 'Im!" said my companion. "No, not 'im. Operatin' is easy, once you understand the apparatus. A organ-grinder could do the rest. Only a question of regulatin' the speed.

"No, I does the effects, and if you want effects done properly you go to the Pink Palace. We'll show you!

"As I say, we've got a quiet lot this week. I wish I had that show. Gives you a chance, that does.

"But 'e missed the lot. Why, with that collision an' that scrap with the pistols, an' that bloke fallin' off the roof, I'd 'ave brought the 'ouse down, and give 'em nerves for a week.

"Not that chap, though. He's a born-tired, I should think. All he worked was the shootin', an' he done that with a clapper—you know, two bits of thin wood. An' then it was half a minute late.

"Now, I've got a little railway accident what sets 'em alight every time. Only a chair, an' a old iron fender I bought for fourpence. But if you work it to rights you can hear the gals scream.

"Motors, too. I tried all sorts of things for motors; rattlin' peas in a tin, shufflin' my feet on the floor; but they wasn't none of 'em no good. Then I thought of sandpaper. Rub it on a bit o' wood, you know; slow at first, then faster an' faster. With that an' a real 'ooter, I've made 'em absolutely jump out o' the way in the front row."

"But how do you study your effects?" I asked. "Have you ever seen a railway collision?"

"That's just where we come in," said "Effects," sticking out his chest. "I ain't seen no collisions, but I know jolly well what one sounds like. So I tries all sorts of things, rattlin' iron an' droppin' weights, till I lands on the chair an' fender. An' I bet any man what's 'eard a collision'd say 'e never 'eard anything like it.

"Frinstance, that bloke fallin' off that roof. Their man didn't work it at all, but week 'fore last we 'ad that film.

"Now I ain't never 'eard a body fall off a roof, but I know 'ow it'd sound if I did; an' I works it this way. I takes my boots off be'ind the screen an' goes 'alfway up a ladder an' jumps down on the boards in my socks—wallop. Just a nice dull note, you know, and just at the right second, too.

"You come along to the Pink Palace next week if you want to see films really worked. We've got some good 'uns comin'.

"There's a cowboy drama, with shootin', an' there's 'The Fisherman's Daughter,' with some fine sea scenes an' waves an' rocks. I've got that all right, I think, with a 'air brush an' some silver sand on a tea tray.

"An' there's a comic, with a soda water siphon that I've been workin' on all the week. An' the 'Battle of Alma.' I use a bugle there. Stuff a 'ankerchief in it, you know, to give the distance."

He rattled through his program, explaining methods and results with a fine enthusiasm. I pictured him sitting alone, in his bedroom perhaps, long after his patrons were in bed, practising cataracts and thunderstorms, trumpeting elephants, and soda water siphons. And I was glad I did not live next door.

"There's one thing worryin' me though," he went on. "You see, I saw some of next week's films at the agents, an' there's a comic circus act with a donkey. An' the donkey brays. You can see it plain as anything, right in the middle of the picture.

"Well, you couldn't let a chance like that go by, could you? 'Course not. But some'ow I can't get that bray right. I've tried an' tried, with squeakers an' things, but it's no use. It ain't bad, mind, but there's something wrong somewheres. You listen."

He stopped under a lamp-post, wrapped his hands round his mouth, and screwed up his eyes. Then brayed in a way to make a jackass jealous; looked round at me for my opinion, and brayed again.

" 'Taint so dusty," he said, "but there's something wrong. It ain't the real thing some'ow."

"I think it's a little too short on the 'hee' and too long on the 'haw'," I suggested.

"P'raps that's it," he agreed; and solemnly tried again. "I believe you've got it," he said. "I'm much obliged. That's been worryin' me. I've tried an' tried till I fair ached. But I believe you've got it.

"I'm going down 'ere," he added, "so I'll wish you goodnight, an' thanks very much. I'm off 'ome to 'ave another pop at that 'ee-'aw." And he disappeared into the night.

I stopped at the corner a while to light up, and presently from down the street came a challenging bray. But I thought it was still a little too short on the "hee."

The Nursemaid

More to rest myself than because I was thirsty (Ah, say you, but you did have one? To which I make answer: Two, my friend, two!), more, I say, to rest than to drink, I lifted the latch of the "Roebuck, by Arthur Kipple," and rapped on the bar.

Presently I put down the blue mug and looked round the parlour. In the shadows by the cold fireplace a carter sat with dog and whip; and "Grmph!" he said to me. I said I thought so too, and hoped it would keep fine for it.

Mr. Kipple was more talkative, but strangely at sea for a landlord. Would chatter of crops and things. How a good yoke of bullocks at Stamford Fair, or how a score of ewes?

True, I carried a ground-ash and a fair powdering of dust; but I had not seen any live cattle for seven long months, and my complexion was about as bucolic as a boiled suet pudding, plain.

With the emptying of the second mug there fell upon my soul a sweet and cloistral peace. The sun shone, the birds sang; the landlord, finding I knew nothing of beeves, snored; somewhere afar off a hen laid an egg, and told the whole cosmic system what a beautiful egg it was. And all that on cider from the wood at twopence the mug. Three mugs, one millennium.

There were three newspapers in the bar. (But, say you, are we getting near the Nursemaid? Patience, dear reader, and all will be well. We shall meet her before the story be done; for that is the purpose of the story.)

There were, I say, three newspapers; and I picked them up like a fool and read in them. And one said that this world was a miserable, ill-fashioned world; and one said that it was as fine a world as ever there was, but for the Government; and one said it was a rotten old world, Government and all, and ought to be sunk at the bottom of the sea, Government and all.

Now, my boots were white with the dust of the road, and my soul was glad within me; so that I felt I could write an epic poem if only I had a subject.

Therefore I threw fourpence at the landlord, ground the newspapers under my heel, and went out into the sun again, ready for dragons or devils nine feet high. 'Twas most excellent cider.

Consider, first, that for half a year I had lived in the mud somewhere between Aldgate Pump and the Brompton Oratory.

Consider, moreover, that the sun was still high, that I should not see Charing Cross again for 17 hours, that (nay, but the Nursemaid, say you ... My dear reader, say I, if I promise you, on my honour, one nursemaid, will you shut up? Good! And now I've forgotten the last thing I was going to suggest for your consideration).

But consider these things, and the mood is forgiven. Have *you* never wished to write poetry?

Perhaps a mile I walked, then sat on a gate and smoked a pipe, and got to work on the epic. But desire outshone performance, and I sucked my pencil and reduced the epic to a threnody, and the threnody to a sonnet. I really would write a sonnet, a new and original sonnet. Not to a thrush's egg, or a myosotis, or a girl, or a sunset; but a sonnet to something bright. My pipe, for instance.

So I began, "O, Pipe"; crossed that out, and started again, "Oh, Pipe." Yet it would not come. Perhaps a fresh opening would be more fruitful. "When from thy bowl—"; much better, this.

When from thy bowl the purple vapours rise
Like incense ...

Like incense—incense burned—burned—ah!

Like incense burned before some something shrine,

(We'll fill in the blanks presently.)

An offering to the drunken god of wine.

That came all in one lump, so I expect I've read it somewhere.

"The next line," I said aloud, "must rhyme with 'rise.' Let's see; cries, dies, prize, lies, sighs."

I often think I hear Young Bacchus sighs.

Not so bad. "Bacchus sighs" is awkward, but still—

"Young man," said a voice from over the hedge. "Young man, catch a-hold of this 'ere ban'box, will you?"

The muse climbed up a tree.

Beauty in distress, thought I; and dropped from the gate into the field. There, sitting on a battered tin trunk at the edge of the ditch, was a young girl, all dressed in sober black. There was the bandbox, too, lying in the damp bottom of the ditch.

"Catch a-hold of that there ban'box, young man; there's a love." So I did, and sat down beside her.

"I s'pose you ain't goin' my way," she asked; "over by Four Ways Junction? These two boxes is 'eavy, an' my boy ain't turned up, an' I'm that cramped squattin' 'ere, you can't think."

"Is it an elopement?" I asked. The girl laughed long and loud.

"If you like," she said. "Elopement! Oh, crumbs. No, young man, it ain't. I done a bunk, that's what. You goin' to Four Ways with me? I can't manage both these 'ere boxes. It's only a matter of two miles or so, an' down 'ill. There's a love!"

"But your young man?" I asked. "Suppose we meet him."

"Oh, 'im!" said the girl. " 'E don't matter. Promised to be 'ere at two, an' it's nigh on four now. Reckon 'e's scared. You see, I done a bunk. I bin 'idin' in the 'edge waitin' for my boy, 'cos I reckon they'll be lookin' for me. You ain't seen a long, lanky woman with nippers an' a curly dog, 'ave you? That's 'er. If she tries to stop me now, I'll— I'll fight 'er. The ole cat, so there!

"P'raps they ain't found out yet," she mused. "But when they do, oh, Chris'mas!"

I had a hazy recollection of something called compounding a felony, and fenced for further particulars before I committed myself to the tin trunk.

"Well, young man, it's like this," said the girl. "I done a bunk-a-doodle-ido. See? I'm the nursemaid at the Vic'ridge, eighteen pound a year, two black frocks, all found an' no beer. One Sunday a month, an' one evenin' a fortnight, after the kids 'as gone to bed. See?

"That's all right. Nothink wrong with that. An' the curit ain't so bad, an' 'is missis, pore dear. But 'e's got a sister what lives with 'im. Miss Agather. Long an' lean an' 'ungry. An' she wears glasses on a chain.

"Found 'er turnin' out my boxes last Sunday. The ole cat. An' do you reckon a nursemaid with three kids to look after ought by rights to 'ave to clean stair-rods an' door-'andles, an' 'elp wash up, an' go to church three times on Sunday, an' then come out before the sermon in the mornin' to peel the 'taters for dinner? An' spend my evenin' off takin' round notes about St. Monica's Guild? 'The walk'll do you good,' she says. So I done a bunk. D'you blame me?"

If the facts were as stated, I did not; and was getting ready to bear off the tin trunk when wheels came round the corner.

"Bob down, young man, bob down," said the nursemaid. "They got a 'orse an' trap … Oh, it's all right. It's my boy. Cheero, Albert! 'Ere I am." The trap stopped, and Albert climbed the gate.

"Who's that?" he asked, looking at me.

"It's all right, ole love," said the girl. "Friend of mine. If you 'adn't come pretty quick we was goin' to elope together. Ain't 'e nice?"

Albert said nothing, but lifted the trunk over the gate, and stowed it under the seat. Then lifted the girl over, and the bandbox; and by the time I reached the road the trap was turning.

"S'long, young man," called the girl. "If you see that long, lanky ole geezer, tell 'er Master Archibald wants some new vests, an' there was a piller slip short in the wash last week; an' Miss Mabel's—"

The rest was dust and the crunch of wheels, and I went back to my sonnet. But the muse was snoring in the topmost branches.

Wrigglesworth

It is laid down in the laws of suburban etiquette that before they may speak to each other two strangers must travel side by side, in the same carriage, night and morning, for eight years. Should one lose his train in the fifth year, they must start all over again.

On some railways, I believe, six years is the limit, but those are fast lines.

It took Wrigglesworth about one hour to get intimate with me; and now I cannot dodge him.

In the beginning, I remember, I trod on his foot at the booking-office; and he said it was his fault, and I said it was mine, and he said his foot had no business to be where it was, and I said neither had my foot.

He insisted, however, that I was not to mention it, that it had not hurt him in the least, that there was nothing to be sorry about, that he had hardly noticed it, and so on and so on, right up the stairs, right along the platform, and right up to Charing Cross.

This was six months ago, and now when he sees me afar off he waves his newspaper, or flaps his handkerchief in the manner of a Sunday-school treat.

Yesterday morning I saw him ploughing his way through the crowd on the platform, and not feeling in a conversational mood, I incontinently fled. But he caught me up.

"Lovely morning, isn't it?" he said. "This'll do the crops good. They want it, too. Splendid weather! What do you think of Huerta?"

"I don't," I answered. "I am admiring that apple-blossom in the stationmaster's garden."

"Ah, well, perhaps you're right," he answered. "Been for your holidays yet?"

"Not this year's," I replied. "In fact, I was thinking about them when you came along."

He settled himself more comfortably in his corner. Here was common ground at last.

"And where do you think of going?" he asked.

"No idea yet," I said. "I rather fancy Cornwall or Stornoway. Or I might go into Sussex." Wrigglesworth became dreadfully earnest at once. He touched the tip of his left thumb with his right forefinger in the manner of one who says "Firstly."

"Let me give you a bit of advice," he said. "Don't go to Sussex. Relaxing. No good." He leaned heavily against me and looked me full in the eyes. "And don't go to Stornoway," he said; adding in a very low whisper, lest there should be any Stornoway men in the carriage, "Drainage, you know. Rotten! I've got a brother-in-law who once spent a holiday in the Kyles of Bute—have you ever been to the Kyles of Bute?"

"Only to one of them," I admitted. "The one on the left as you go from here." But he swept on.

"Cornwall, now. That's all right. Fine, bracing climate. Very historic spot, too. Ever been there before?"

"Once," I told him. "I stayed at Chipping Norton."

"But Chipping Norton isn't in Cornwall, is it?" he asked.

"Then it must have been Chipping Sodbury," I said; "or Chipping Ongar. It was Chipping Something."

"I expect you're thinking of Chippenham," said Wrigglesworth.

"I've been to Cornwall three times," he continued. "Fine country. Fine people. Last time I went we stopped at Trelawny. Fine old town. Built by King Arthur, you know. Or was it Alfred? I forget. But it's awfully historic. Named after the Trelawny man. Him the fifty million Cornishmen wanted to know the reason why about in the poem. Or was it fifty thousand? I forget."

"Split the difference," I suggested.

"But it's chockful of relics and things," continued Wrigglesworth. "I've got a guide book at home I could lend you if you like.

"And legends! Why, they've got a stone there, outside the town, that's called Alfred's Cushion. Supposed to have been left over when the church was built. And there's the print of King Arthur's knees in it where he gave thanks."

"Well," I began, "I never thought Alfred was a hard man."

"Not Alfred," said Wrigglesworth, "Arthur. That's why it's called Aethelstane in the old legends. Arthur's Stone. See?"

"I see," I replied. "But you'd have to give thanks a long time to wear dents in a rock, wouldn't you? This Arthur person must have been frightfully hard on his trousers."

"Ah!" said Wrigglesworth. "You see, they wore armour in those days. And there's another thing you must see when you get down there.

"There's a hill and a big flat rock at the top, just the shape of a cake. That's called the Simmel Cake, because the legend says that during the War of the Roses—I wish I'd got that book with me—What's-his-name, Perkin Warbeck, used to meet his followers there. Or was it the Young Pretender? Anyway, it's worth going to see. Just like a cake."

"Currant or plain?" I asked.

"Plain," said Wrigglesworth solemnly. "Just a plain round cake. But if you'll let me know when you're going, I'll let you have a list of the places of interest in the neighbourhood."

"That's very good of you," I said seriously. "But about these legends. I don't want to go there and be diddled."

"Oh, I think they are genuine enough," said Wrigglesworth. "True, some of them are a bit—well, far fetched; but you must remember they go back to the days of miracles."

"That's what makes me suspicious," I said. "Take Southend. Now down at Southend they show you the actual spot where King Canute told the sea to go away. And you can see for yourself that it has gone away and never come back again.

"Well, on the face of it, that looks genuine enough; but you think! There wasn't any Southend in Canute's time, was there?"

"That's true," said Wrigglesworth. "Still, I think you can trust these Cornish legends. You see, Cornwall's well established; but Southend—"

"That's just it," I protested. "Here are you trying to persuade me to go to Cornwall on the strength of legends, and then you tell me that you think I can trust 'em.

"You can't remember whether it was fifty thousand or fifty million Cornishmen who wanted to know the reason why about this show. And on such flimsy evidence you would drag me right across England to see a stone like a big muffin where Barclay Perkins and Miss Warbeck used to meet the Young Pretender. It isn't good enough, Wrigglesworth," I said. He was not a bit put out.

"I'm sure you'd find it infinitely more interesting than Stornoway," he said. "I may be wrong about those men and the reason why, but I never was much good at figures. Anyway, I'll bring the book up tomorrow. Here's my station.

"I'm almost certain it was fifty thousand," he said from the platform. "How does it go? 'Fifty thousand horse and foot, going to Table Bay.' That's it. You'd find it awfully interesting, really."

The Goldfish

Since I kept "tiddler brats" in a jam-jar, feeding them on pieces of worm and breadcrumbs, from which they died, my study of ichthyology has ceased. Imagine, then, my concern at receiving the following letter from a small nephew whom I patronise:

Dear Unk thank you very much for the nice goldfishes you gave me the goldfishes are ill and one is very ill. It will not swim but floats and when I push it under with my finger it comes up again and dear Unk what do you feed goldfishes on?

Dad says they suck the oxgin out of the water with their jills but they wont eat ants eggs. Dear Unk do you think this ants egg is good?

I have looked at goldfishes in dads book and it says goldfishes see Carp and it says carp often live to 500 years old and were considered a delcacy by the ancients.

I have given them some watercress and a snail and another thing and some pebbles to make it like a pond but they are ill and do tell me are flies good for goldfishes. There are not many flies here yet but I think I could get some.

And dad doesnt know anything about goldfishes and he says your uncle ought to have more sense your affect. neph.

SNORKS.

P.S. The ants egg is in the envelope in the corner. The fishes dont take any notice of them. There is 2d. worth your

SNORKS.

Let it be written to my credit that I heard the call afar off, and hurried to the rescue of those unfortunate goldfishes.

The enclosure I could not find. We have had some warm weather lately, and maybe there is an ant belonging to me at the G.P.O.

An inspection of the proffered food being thus impossible, I had to resort to books. I read up the secret history of *Carassius auratas*, his life and loves, his manners and customs.

I turned up the Carp, its mythology, its origin, its place in natural history and music. I read a column on carp-worship, a shorter article on the true inwardness of the goldfish.

Then, in an encyclopædia, I found succour.

"The Carp," it said, "is capable of living out of water for several hours. Its food is either vegetable or animal."

No good trying fish-hooks, then; or tenpenny nails. Perhaps a nice turnip or a chump chop— Vegetable or animal! And then the book went straight on to Carpathians and Carpets.

Something had to be done. That night I lay abed watching three gasping goldfish swimming languidly round and round in a glass globe, stopping here and there to stare at me with big, melancholy eyes, to open and shut their mournful, drooping mouths, dumb things striving to speak.

Next day I went to a fish shop, but that was no good. They only dealt with dead fish, so I said I'd call again presently. Later I rang up the Zoo, but the keeper of the carp had gone to dinner.

Then I remembered the little dark shop where they sell glass eyes and Dusty Millers and catgut and stuffed seagulls.

I expected a bearded old gentleman with gleaming spectacles, fresh from sewing up a stuffed lion in the back shop; but there came instead a bright, dapper young man, quick moving and businesslike.

"My little nephew—" I began.

"Ah, yes, of course," said the young man sympathetically. That helped me a lot.

"Goldfish," I started again. "I've bought him some goldfish, and they're sick. What do you do?"

"Ah, goldfish," repeated the shopkeeper. "Yes, I know all about goldfish, but I really can't say that I know anything *about* them. I could stuff them for you, and mount them life like."

"Not yet," I said. "Perhaps in a day or two, if all else fails. But not yet."

The young man meditated.

"Um! Sick, are they? Pale like?"

"That's it," I said. "That's just it. They swim round and round, and stare for hours at nothing, and then swim round and round again. No interest in life. No appetite. And twopenn'orth of good ants' eggs going to waste. Can't you do something?"

"Not much in my line," said he. "But I have got a nephew myself—" (dashing the tears from his eyes) "—and I'll see what I can do for you."

He fetched out a fat, dusty volume, and read aloud:

"Gold. Golders Green. Goldbeater's skin. Here we are, Goldfish." He marked the place with his forefinger, and beamed up at me.

"The goldfish," he said, "is a freshwater fish in the physostomatous division."

"Thanks, awfully," I said.

"A type of the family Cyprinidae," he continued.

"Ah, that accounts for it," I remarked. "The man with the barrow never said anything about that. I bought them off a barrow, you know. He said they were 22 carat, and they certainly looked nice and shiny; but now I understand the gold's wearing off. Can you do anything?"

" 'Fraid not," said the young man. "You see, without knowing the fish I cannot diagnose."

"Doesn't it say anything about their grub?" I asked anxiously.

"No," he said, after a long search. "Not a word. What do you feed them on?"

"That's what I'm trying to find out," I answered. "You see, there were no printed instructions given with them, no book of rules. And Snorks, my nephew, you know, writes that he has tried watercress and ants' eggs, but they only turn up their noses. D'you know if the ants' eggs should be served raw or boiled; and if the latter, hard or soft?"

The young man drummed his fingers on the counter.

"Let's try carp," he said. "Ah, here we are! Family so-and-so. Genus so-and-so. Mainly vegetarian. Eats larvae and worms occasionally."

"Grand!" I shouted. "Fine! I believe you've saved their lives. Can you let me have sixpennyworth of larvae at once? Make it a bob's worth while you're at it. Snorks will be awfully pleased."

And then, just as I was writing out a telegram to my nephew, he told me there were 75 million varieties of larvae in the world. And you only got a very few for sixpence.

"Then is there no medicine to make sick goldfish well?" I asked. "Nothing to make them eat worms? We've got tons of worms in our garden. Meaty ones, too. A tonic, now; something to take in water before meals, or on a piece of sugar."

Well, we searched Culpepper and Izaak Walton, and books on fly-fishing, and the Home Physician, but all to no purpose; and I went home hopeless, fearful of the night and what might happen.

But before I went the young man extracted from me a promise that, all other things failing, he should have the stuffing of the pets.

I believe now that he could have saved them all the time. What will a man not do for money!

This morning I had a picture postcard from Snorks. Thus:

Dear Unk another of the goldfishes has come to the top that makes two the others looked bad and dad said they were on there last legs so I swoped them with Arthur Bailey for a bone arrow and some cigarette pictures. So no more now your affect. neph.

SNORKS.

And I thought he was sitting up all night with them!

The Stores

With the most hazy ideas of my duties in the matter, I consented some eleven months ago to become a godfather. Archibald was to be the child's name.

I protested, of course. Pointed out that all the Archibalds I had ever known were shady characters. Collected newspaper cuttings to prove it.

"Archibald Merthyr, described as an actor"; "Archibald Tydfil, one of a well-known Continental gang"; and so on. But they went their own silly way.

"He'll be a nut," I said, "with stick-up collars and horseshoes on his waistcoat. Don't say I didn't tell you. And, anyway, whatever you call him, he'll be Fatty at school, or Podge, or Snookums. Serve you right."

But Archibald he was and is; and I had to condone the crime and hold the baby. Tomorrow he is one year old, and I have to signify the same in the usual manner.

So I went to the Stores; one of those great establishments with a double-barrelled name, like Sankey and Moody or Barnum and Bailey.

There was a man dressed like an Emperor just inside the door, and as I approached he genuflected until I heard his corsets creak.

"I want a present," I said.

"Straight along," said the Emperor, "until you come to the animalculae department. Then take the lift as far as it goes, and ask again." And he genuflected some more.

Halfway down that avenue of counters I began to wish I had brought some sandwiches with me. There was a blister on my heel, too; but I struggled bravely on.

As I sank fainting on the eighth milestone, a gentleman approached rubbing his hands. "Doctor Livingstone, I presume," said I, and held out my hand.

"Rest room on Floor M," he answered. "Drug department, third on your right past the aquaria. Consulting physician on the mezzanine floor, but I think he's gone home."

"Home!" I echoed. "I shall never see home again. Tell them," I said, "tell them that I died— Look here, I want a present, not a walking tour. Present department, quick."

"Straight along and take the lift," he said, and disappeared into the blue distance.

I got there, and they were having a medal struck. A tsar with a drum major's wand met me, breathing frostily.

"Hallo, Etookishook," I whispered. "Don't the days draw in! Where's the Aurora Borealis?"

"Borealis department, Block G, Floor Y, between the bottled beer and Rembrandt prints."

"No, you don't!" I answered. "I've come all the way from London to this department, and what I have I hold. Presents are what I'm after. Lead on, Macduff!"

"Third right, fourth left, straight on," said the tsar, and it was so. There was the present department, just as I got my second wind.

"And what sort of present?" asked an expensively dressed young man.

"For a boy," I said. "A boy named Archibald, but that isn't his fault. A birthday present."

"Ah, yes," said the assistant. "And how old is the young man?"

"This is his second birthday," I answered. "So he'll be just one, won't he?"

"Two, I think," said the salesman.

"One," I persisted. "You see, the day he was born was his first birthday, and this— If you don't believe me, you try your ready reckoner department. Floor Z, Block X, Counter B, and then the third on your left past the second pillar box. Hope you have fine weather."

"Ah, well," he said, "if you put it like that—one, of course. Now a present for a boy of one. Let's see, let's see. Rather difficult, isn't it? But, of course, he'll grow up."

"That is our intention," I said. "That's what he's for, to grow up. And he's doing it, too. You ought to see him tossing the caber with his bottle, and doing the Gates of Gaza act with his cot. A marvellous youth!"

"Are you his father?" asked the young man.

"No, sir," I answered; "or his name would not have been Archibald. My enthusiasm is purely that of a godparent."

"Ah, a godparent!" said the salesman. "Then you'll want something costly, something lasting. They expect it, you know. Aunts and all that sort of thing usually give a rattle. But a godparent—well, it's up to you. What shall we say?"

"Oh, something about two and eleven three," I said. But he thought that was a joke.

"Miss Vavasour, forward, please," he called, and there swept up to me a goddess in black and smiles. We bowed.

"Beastly crush," I said. "What! Shall we find the stairs and sit out this one? There's a howling mob in the supper room, and all the claret cup's gone."

"A present for a little boy," she answered. "Step this way, please." I tried, but it wasn't a success.

"Now, here's a dainty little thing," said the lady. "Turquoise and silver, with bells and chain. Excellent for the gums. Three eight eleven."

I leaned heavily on the counter.

"Miss De Courcy," I began.

"Miss Vavasour," she corrected.

"Miss Vavasour," I repeated. "I want to talk to you as man to man. I came here to buy a present for a good boy. I want to give him something enduring, something that will remind him of me in the days to come. A teddy bear or an edible Noah's Ark, or a boy scout's outfit.

"I've been led about and up and down until I'm faint with hunger; I've been bullied by half-pay Russian officers who use brilliantine; the soles of my boots are flapping, and I want a shave.

"I've got five shillings in my pocket, and you show me chunks of turquoise."

"Oh, well," she said, "if you've only got five shillings—go along there as far as you can see—"

"Past the telegraph pole?" I asked, shading my eyes.

"Yes, and straight on through the Dutch Garden till you come to the swimming baths. Then ask again."

I thanked her, and started off.

"If I get out alive," I said, "I'll send you some chocolates."

Within an hour I was lying on a sofa in the toy department R to Z, while a tall damsel laid teddy bears at my feet.

"This one," she said, "is four and eleven. If you squeeze it there it says 'Moo.' "

"But that's a cow," I protested. "Bears don't say 'Moo.' "

"This one does," said the lady. "Shall I send it?"

"Send it by all means," I said. "And you can send me as well if you like. I'd like to see the old place once more."

"Straight down there," said the damsel, "third right, third left, second right again. Then take the lift. One penny change. Pleasant journey …"

The Emperor opened the door and threw rice at me.

"Dear old London!" I cried. "Dear old London! Not altered much after all. I wonder if they'll know me at home." Then I bought a paper to see the date.

The Gypsy

There was a little pain, like a thin silver wire, that ran up one side of my head and down the other. Not all the time, but chiefly when I put on my overcoat.

I took it for neuralgia, and carried my overcoat on my arm. Mrs. Boddy, and expert in pains, said it was indigestion. She scraped the soapsuds from her arms and peered at me through the steam.

"Yerbs is what you want," she said. "Yerbs. You puts 'em in a pot an' stoos 'em an' stoos 'em, an' you drinks the liquor." Then she went on slopping pyjamas round in the froth.

The doctor was nearer the truth. "Overwork," he said, and I liked him for it. I think overwork is a fine complaint. You know you are getting something for your money. If he had said overfeeding or over-anything else, I should have changed my doctor. But overwork—I felt quite proud of myself.

"Take a week off and change all your habits of life," he said. "Go a-walking or cycling. Go hop picking or whatever's in season. A week's rest will put you right. And this, night and morning."

Of course I couldn't take a week; one must think of one's country. But I took a day, and sang out of the carriage window as the train hurried me away to the sweet gorse and the bright young bracken of the little hills.

All I lacked was a tin trumpet to blow as we passed the up-trains, heavy with men in collars scurrying to work.

Slowly, because a new view opened up at each step, and there were violets hid in the bracken, I climbed to the top where that ancient road runs from Canterbury to the West.

Under my feet the fallen pine needles crackled; the wind that came from the sea was full of sweet smells; there was a thrush in the thicket, and away down in the woody valley a cuckoo called.

There I turned my face London-wards, and addressed all you, with your noses to the grindstones. "Go it, you silly chumps," I called. "Keep the pot a-boiling." I was feeling better already.

The road ran along the roof ridge of a fair country, close up under the sky; and beneath last year's dead undergrowth I found bluebells bent under the heavy dew, and cowslips and late primroses.

From far down in the hollow came a sound of wood chopping, and the honk of a motor on the unseen highway.

And so to a clearing, a wide space in the track where the sun came through without shadows. There on a thrown beech I rested for a pipe's length, and blew smoke at the dancing gnats.

Through the warm silence came a sound of song; a young voice, full of gladness and freedom. Then the dull thump of slow hoofs, and the singer came in view; a small figure on a fat white horse that sometimes ambled along, and sometimes stayed to nibble at the sweet grass by the track side.

As the rider crossed a bar of light I saw her to be a young girl, fifteen perhaps, sitting astride and whacking her steed with a green branch. Her song I knew not, but certainly she was a gypsy; a Lovell or a Herne, one of Borrow's own.

Said the youthful earl to the gypsy girl,
    As the moon was casting her silver shine,
"Brown little lady, Egyptian lady,
    Let me kiss those sweet red lips of thine."

Somehow that did not seem to fit the wild tune that floated through the glade. There was a gay lilt to it, a vigour and freedom, a breath of the open heath.

Such a picture in such a setting does not come often to the town dweller. I watched her as she passed through the splashes of light where the gaps overhead let the sun through; a brown maiden with a face the colour of autumn beech leaves; hair blowing free, and bare legs drumming on the horse's flanks.

She pulled up at sight of me, and slid lightly to the ground. Slung round her neck were two limp rabbits, tied by their hind feet.

"Tell your fortune, pretty gentleman," she said, and there was a whine in her voice. "Tell you fortune for a piece of silver."

"No, thank you," I answered, "but if you like you may tell me your own fortune. What is your name? It ought to be Meg Merrilies."

" 'Tain't Nosey Parker, anyway," said the pretty little girl. "Tell you for tuppence."

I signified that negotiations were now at an end, and she returned to the whining tone.

"Only a copper or two before you go, pretty gentleman. Won't break you."

"Where's the camp?" I asked.

" 'Bout 'alf a mile," she said. "I'll show you. Farver's there, an' my young bruvver. 'E's got five fingers an' a fum on each 'and. 'E'll show you for a tanner."

I declined this treat.

"And what do you do for a living?" I asked.

"You don't 'alf want to know nothink, you don't!" said the gypsy maiden. "Are you the school board man?"

I reassured her, and ostentatiously counted some coppers.

"Farver does all sorts," she said, presently. "Mends chairs, makes baskets, an' cradles an' things, an' does odd jobs."

"And are you a real gypsy?" I asked.

"Gypsy!" she said indignantly. "I'll 'ave you know we're respectable. We live in a 'ouse in the winter, we do, after the 'oppin'. In our own 'ouse. Gypsy!"

I apologised, and rattled the money again.

"And what do you do?" I pursued.

"Fruit pickin', sellin' ferns an' primrose roots, an' tells fortunes for mugs. Tell yours, if you like."

"Do people still have their fortunes told?" I asked.

"Sometimes," she said. "If they don't, I tell 'em I got to take some money 'ome or else farver 'll bash me."

"And would he?" I asked.

"Who? 'Im?" she exclaimed. "Not 'im! You goin' to give us those coppers?"

"Just a minute," I said. While we were slashing at my romantic canvas we might as well tear the whole thing down. "What was that song you were singing before you saw me?"

She took the coppers, moistened them, sprang astride her horse again, and kicked it in the ribs. Then broke again into that wild gypsy air:

For we all go to work 'cep' farver,
'E stops at 'ome all day,
Sittin' by the fire—

"Cl'k, come up, Joey!"

—With a pot o' four ale,
Smokin' 'is ten-inch clay, ta-ra-ra!

"Thank you very much," I said. "And now will you kindly go away? Go about a hundred yards away, and stop there. You look better at a distance."

"All right, face," said the maiden. Then, in the manner of one exhibiting strange beasts: "Barmy on the crumpet. Quite barmy. Fell out o' the pram when 'e was little, an' never smiled again. Git over, Joey!"

The Nightingale

Apart from his love of nature, Darbyshire is, I think, a decent enough fellow; but he will gas about the rural amenities of the potty little place where he lives.

When I see him rubbing his hands on the platform in the morning—rubbing them together, I mean—I know that a heron flew over his chimney pot the night before, or that he has discovered the spoor of a Red Admiral on the lawn.

He was doing this on Wednesday; and when he said "Good morning" his ears were the limit of his smile.

"Hallo, Darbyshire!" I said. "Don't tell me your Gloire de Dijon has flowered already, or that you've found a caterpillar of the Purple Crested Death or Glory Moth."

"Ah, you will have your little joke," said Darbyshire indulgently. "But this time—" And the corners of the smile pushed his ears violently back.

"Then there's a tomtit's nest in your shaving mug," I said; "or the aspidistra has littered."

"No, you funny ass," said Darbyshire. "But if you'd like to come round tonight, about eight, you shall see for yourself."

I tried several ways to draw him, but got no more than that.

"If you don't soon tell somebody," I said, "you'll go pop, old man. Your steam's mounting and mounting, you were never designed to stand all that pressure, and if you grin any more the top of your head will come off."

"Tonight at eight," he answered.

"And then we'll write to the paper about it," I said. "Sign it Paterfamilias or Rus in Urbe, like you did about the big maggot of

Stow-in-the-Wold, and the Boxing Day periwinkle on Wimbledon Common.

" 'Sir, I should like to place on record an event which I think is unique in the annals of the flora and fauna of Streatham,' and so on. 'Flora and fauna' will fetch any editor, you know. It's Latin, like *E pluribus unum* and *Quant. suff.*"

"What a fine back-chat comedian you'd make!" said Darbyshire. "All you want is a partner to smack your face at intervals."

"But tell me this," I said. "Is it a glow-worm? Because if it is I shan't come. I once saw a glow-worm, and it didn't live up to the advertisements."

"Perhaps it wasn't trying," said Darbyshire. "Anyway, this is not a glow-worm. Tonight at eight, then. By-bye!"

There was a strange hush about Darbyshire's place that evening. He led me up and down the garden for a time, pointing out the sticks where the gladioli and dahlias and things would shortly be; and then he broke the news.

"I was sitting out here Sunday evening," he said, "smoking a final pipe, when I heard in those laurels at the bottom of the vicar's garden—a nightingale." He stepped back a pace to watch the effect of this.

"Good heavens!" I said. "You don't mean it."

"Unmistakably a nightingale," said Darbyshire; "on Sunday evening at 9.15, May 10th. It sang for a good fourteen minutes."

"Strange," I said. "But anyway, I shouldn't let it worry me. Perhaps no one else heard it. Have you complained to the vicar?"

"It was there again Monday night and last night," he went on, "and I thought you'd like to hear it. We could sit out here, you know, and I've got some cigars."

I pressed his hand in silence, and he went in to get the chairs.

"Perhaps we'd better not talk," said Darbyshire. "They are shy birds, and easily frightened."

"Mum's the word," I agreed, and for a while there was no sound but the crackling of the saltpetre in my cigar. Then I thought of something.

"Look here, Darbyshire," I whispered, "when this thing starts up, are you going to quote Keats? Because if you do I shall trot out Omar. Or if you like I'll toss you for first pop."

"Sh-sh!" said Darbyshire. "You're making the chair creak."

And so we sat for maybe six or seven hours. I was pins and needles all over when Darbyshire asked me if I knew the time.

"Don't strike a match," he said hurriedly, "perhaps it's just about to begin."

"It smells awfully late, or awfully early," I said. "Can't you tell from the Pleiades? Oh, there you are! Orion's just stepping across your chimney pot, and the people next door are going to bed, or else getting up. Do you think it's tonight still, or is tonight last night?"

"If you don't shut up I'll kill you," said my host. So we sat and sulked for another hour or two.

"Doesn't seem to be coming," said Darbyshire at last. "I'm sorry."

"It's these cigars," I said, and yawned elaborately. "Still, I've had a very pleasant weekend, and if it does come off, you know where I live. I believe you've done your best, Darbyshire, but I think you ought to have fixed things up with the vicar—"

"Sh-sh-sh!" he hissed. "Listen!"

And sure enough, in the distance we heard a plaintive piping, a few rusty bars of music.

"The nightingale," whispered Darbyshire. "It's further away tonight, but I think that makes it sweeter. Listen!"

I could not see him, but I knew his chest was stuck out, his thumbs in his armholes. This was his bird, his show, and after my scoffing he had a right to swell about it. The song ceased, and this was Darbyshire's cue.

… thou, light-winged Dryad of the trees,
In some melodious plot
Of beechen green, and shadows numberless,
Singest of summer in full-throated ease.

This was followed by a tremendous sigh.

"Tell me, Darbyshire," I said, "does a drowsy numbness pain your sense as though of hemlock you had drunk? Does it?"

"Shut up, you infernal ass," said he, hoarsely.

"Because," I continued, "they're putting on a new record … Ah, there it is. Bridal Chorus! Lum, tum-ti-tum."

There was a painful silence, but I wasn't going to be done out of my quote.

"Now more than ever, Darbyshire, seems it rich to die," I said; "to cease, Darbyshire, upon the midnight with no pain."

He got up and kicked his chair over.

"I wish you wouldn't chuck your beastly cigar ends all over the lawn," he said.

"*Your* beastly cigar ends," said I. "And now, old chap," I added, "if you don't talk about this no one will know. Sort of thing that might happen to any man. Unreliable things, farthingales. You ought to have made an appointment.

The farthingale that in the branches sang,
An, whence and whither flown again, who knows?

"I said I'd work it in. And now, if you'll lend me a clean collar, I can just catch the last workman's up to town. Don't the nights draw in!"

The Excursion

Not affluence, but a vigorous and earnest Sunday School treat drove me to the hot cushions of a first, when I would fain have been honest and travelled in a wooden third. But they were not to be dodged that way; and no sooner was I settled and the blinds drawn on the sunny side, than the door opened, and a lump of the treat, about twenty of it, bundled into the carriage, and we were off.

For some time they busied themselves trying to make the two open windows frame ten heads apiece. In this process I was considerably stamped upon, and someone dropped a slice of lunch, jam downwards, on my trousers.

Cheering signal boxes and platelayers soon began to pall on some of them; and one, a girl with a freckled nose, gave an exhibition horizontal-bar act on the luggage rack.

Built for light packages only, this creaked horribly, and I prodded the child in the calf, advising her to desist. Whereat she turned and spoke to me, standing on the company's plush upholstery.

"Mind who you're jabbin' of," she said; "and keep your stick to yourself."

I explained that my concern was for her safety, also pointing out that the cushions were meant to sit on.

"You ought to talk, you did," she answered. " 'Ad your feet on 'em when we come in." She turned to the framed notice to passengers.

"Liable to a penalty of forty shillin's, or a munf, you are," she said. "So *you* didn't ought to talk." Here I found a champion in a little close-cropped boy, very shiny as to the face.

"An' you didn't ought to talk, neiver, Daisy Perkins, so there," he yelled. "You're a-standin' on 'em."

"Well, an' what if I am?" said Daisy. "We're wiv a 'scursion, an' we can do what we like. 'E ain't wiv a 'scursion, so there. An' you mind your own bus'ness, Jimmy Dark."

There was a scramble for the windows again as the train slowed into a station, and Daisy and Jimmy were soon taking the lead in that famous chorus which tells how "We're all a-goin' to Rye 'Ouse, we're all a-goin' to Rye 'Ouse, we're all a-goin' to Rye 'Ouse, so 'Ip-'ip-'ip-'ooray!"

This was manifestly absurd, for Rye House is on quite another line; and when they had chanted their slogan about one hundred and seventy times I pointed out the error to Jimmy Dark.

"Oh, that don't matter!" said Jimmy. "You 'as to sing that when you're on a 'scursion. Don't matter where you're goin' really. Besides, we're goin' to Burn'am Beeches, an' you can't sing 'We're all a-goin' to Burn'am Beeches, can you? It don't fit in, does it?"

He tried it; they all tried it; and after a quarter of an hour of it decided that it couldn't be done.

"You could leave out the word 'all'," I suggested. "Then it would fit, I think." So they tried that. Fifty-seven times they tried that, only to reject it at last in favour of Rye House.

At the next station they changed their minds once more, and expressed a fervent desire to be down home in Dixie. Then came lunch, the untying of great parcels of bread and butter; with much swapping of slices, and handing round of bottles of gaudy drink.

But someone in the corner took too many gulps, and in the scrimmage for the bottle a face got smashed, and another, and another. Daisy was in that, and lost her hair ribbon, whereupon she wailed in a high treble, and laid about her right and left.

Fearing she was mortally injured, I was about to pull the communication cord when her tears suddenly ceased, and she drew a long breath.

"All right, young Ernie," she said, "I 'eard you, an' I'll tell Teacher Maud about you, see if I don't, so there."

"I never said nuffink," protested young Ernie; but Daisy knew better.

"Yes, you did," she said. "I 'eard you. You swore. An' now you'll go to 'ell." She glowed all over as she said it, and evidently derived tremendous satisfaction from this possibility; and all the others looked wide eyed at the young Cassandra, and rounded their mouths and said "Oooo!"

Not so young Ernie. He didn't believe in it. His father had told him it was all swank. He wasn't going, not in those trousers. Besides, where did they get their coal from? All swank, that's what it was.

Daisy saw her chance of squaring accounts getting smaller.

"You will," she said, while the others listened awestruck. "Teacher Maud said so. She told us in a lesson once, so you look out. You swore, an' you'll go, see if you don't."

Young Ernie's faith in his exemption was wavering.

"Coo, what's she know about it?" he sneered. "My farver knows more'n she does. 'E works for the Borough Council, 'e does. 'E says it's all swank."

Then Daisy turned fiercely to me.

"Won't 'e, mister? 'E'll go to 'ell, won't 'e?"

Long ago I had been frightened into bad dreams by this same thing, so I relieved Ernie's mind, to Daisy's great disappointment.

"Not for that he won't," I said; "but he mustn't say it again, because it isn't pretty."

"But Teacher Maud—" protested Daisy.

"I should ask her again if I were you," I said, floundering a little. "I don't suppose she meant it. Besides, on an excursion, you know—" But Daisy would not have it that there were any special terms for excursionists.

She was a bloodthirsty little girl, and was not going to be cheated out of her revenge. Young Ernie had smacked her face, and had said what he should not. And Young Ernie was in for it. Further, I was not a Sunday School teacher, nor did I know everything. She turned from me to the three other little girls, and to them expressed her unshaken belief in Young Ernie's future, while they listened awestruck at the fervour of her hot-gospelling.

Young Ernie had swore, and Young Ernie would go to 'ell, see if he didn't!

But when I left them, Young Ernie, the accused and convicted, was out of the window to the waist, and he was going to Rye 'Ouse, 'Ip-'ip-'ip-'ooray!

Blackmail

A philosopher, inclined by reason of a sluggish liver to look upon the darker side of life, once said that if a dozen men received telegrams telling them to "fly at once, all is discovered," ten of them would fly.

The experiment, I know, was tried upon a celebrated dean, one of the rural variety. He got as far as Calais before his friends could persuade him that the thing was a hoax. But in that case the word "all" had been underlined.

These things flashed through my mind last Thursday evening when I answered the door to a tall smirking man who carried a brown-paper parcel. There was something about him—his grey flannel shirt, perhaps, or his nicely oiled hair, or his blue serge trousers—anyway, my heart sank within me, my whole past life swam before me, my income tax returns sang in my ears. I gulped hard, moistened my lips, and whispered "Come in, constable. Come in."

He wiped one boot on my two by four mat, and came in, still smiling a little, carrying his head in the official manner, squaring his shoulders, and stepping deliberately.

When he had seated himself on the extreme edge of a chair, his parcel between his feet, he placed a hand on either knee, and said, "I see you recognise me, sir. How d'you feel today?"

"I'm sorry," I answered, "but I'm afraid I do not." At which he lengthened his smile a fraction, winked ponderously, and laid a fat forefinger to the side of his nose.

Then, glancing at his parcel, he said, "I've brought back your hat, sir. A little bit damaged, I think, but a nice hot iron will soon make it all right again."

"My hat?" I questioned, in genuine astonishment. "I haven't lost a hat." The policeman smirked still harder, and winked once more so that I heard it click.

"Yes, sir, I think so, sir," he answered. "I don't suppose you've forgotten. Last night, sir." He fumbled with the string of the parcel.

"But I—let me see!—I really don't think I was out last night," I said. "No, I'm sure I wasn't."

"I think so, sir," he answered. " 'Course, we constables see heaps of that sort of thing. Heaps! But you can rely on me, sir. Won't go any further."

Now, believe me, I was *not* out on the previous night. At seven o'clock I was hunting greenfly on the Dorothy Perkins; at eight I was reading; at nine supping; and at ten, fast asleep in bed. And unless I am a sleep walker—

"Will you kindly oblige me by explaining?" I said.

"Lor, sir," said the policeman. "It ain't nothing to be ashamed of. Often happens. Gents gets a bit lively after the Derby, you know. Heaps of 'em. And you was—well, you'd been enjoying yourself same's the rest."

"And where was this?" I asked.

"Trafalgar Square, sir," said he. "I was off duty myself, an' took you in charge. Took care of you, you know. You wasn't half bad neither. Took me an' the driver to get you in the taxi, and then I brought you home here. Taxi cost four an' six, sir, an' a shilling for the driver."

"Oh, so we came home in a taxi, did we?" I said. "I wish I'd been conscious. I love riding in taxis. And where did you find the hat, constable? Was Nelson wearing it, or Gordon?"

"No, sir," he said. "I fished the hat out of one of the fountains. Spoilt the nap, I'm afraid, but a hot iron— An' your name an' address was inside of it, an' that's how I knew where to bring you."

Here I began to see a light.

"Thank you, constable; thank you a thousand times," I said. "How can I ever repay you?"

"Well, sir," said the policeman; "there's the taxicab, six bob, an' two bob for the driver for giving me a hand with you—say half a sovereign out-o'-pocket exes. I leave it to you, sir."

"Cheap," I exclaimed. "Dirt cheap. And now let me have a look at the hat. Ah, there it is! The nights we've had together. The weddings and funerals we've been to. Makes me feel old, constable. I wonder if he fits me still. I suppose you kept this as evidence."

"That's it, sir," he answered. "No harm done, an' nothing to be afraid of. Derby night, you know."

"Ah, constable," I said. "Boys will be boys. Youth must out."

"But, my word, you was a handful," he said, admiringly. "An' the taxi cost eight bob, with half a dollar for the driver on account of you singing an' going on."

I put my hand in my pocket and kept it there, while the policeman's smile spread to right and left.

"Constable," I said, sadly, "you've been had! Fourpence thrown away in bus fares this evening, and a good story gone to pot. I've got an alibi, constable."

The smile faded; he licked his lips and toyed with the faded hat.

"You fished that thing out of the fountain; you read my name and address inside, and you thought I should pay up and be thankful.

"But you're barking up the wrong tree, constable. You've been led away on a false scent. Six months ago I lent that old hat to a friend to wear at a funeral, and I've never seen it since … Shall I open the door for you? No, no! Take the topper, there's a good chap. Wear it for my sake, or have it framed. And goodnight, constable. No offence. Let not the sun go down upon your wrath, you know." He did look the most miserable policeman!

"I'm sorry about all that taxi money," I continued. "Fifteen shillings, wasn't it? And how many men did it take to get me inside? Six? That makes me feel a very devil of a fellow, you know. Well, if you must go, the bottom step's the lowest."

At the gate he found his voice again.

"Been a mistake somewhere," he mumbled. "Hope you won't let it go no further. But I'll swear I took somebody home, and your name was in the hat. S'pose I shan't see my quid any more." And he walked away.

At ten paces he turned back again.

"I s'pose you couldn't let me have your friend's address?" he said.

"Oh, certainly," I answered; and he got out his notebook. "It's No. 84, Trewarnhayle Road—"

"Tre-warn-hayle Road," he said, licking his pencil.

"Exeter," I added.

What he said here doesn't matter, and before I could tell him about the cheap trips he was out of sight.

Travel Talk

With the long, light evenings homework ceases; and my fellow passengers on the 4.38, Prunes and Prisms, freed from their French and "trig," have leisure to entertain me.

Since I made such a pitiful mess of their algebra ("Don't rag the poor man," Prunes had said. "When he went to school algebra wasn't invented."), they have taken to including me in their confidences. Before I choose my carriage, I run my eye along the train seeking the two broad-brimmed straw hats, and on half-holidays the homeward journey seems dull.

Prunes, I should think, is about thirteen, with all the wisdom of forty; Prisms, judging by her dictatorial tone, must be some two or three months older; and from their lips falls glib and biting criticism of those set in authority above them.

Their headmistress, I have learned, is a "dear old chump who means well enough, but—"; while Domino, who takes them in mathematics, is "the limit in freckles."

"And you should see her legs, too! She comes to gym in costume, and of all the awful sights! Broomhandles, absolutely."

All this in a clear, certain voice; with no pretence of secrecy, no recognition of the presence of strangers,

Last evening we talked of summer holidays and parents and things. There must have been a lot of ears burning somewhere.

"Your people fixed anything up?" asked Prunes.

"Don't know," said Prisms. "They haven't told me yet. S'pose it'll be Eastbourne again. Three times running that'll be. The guv'nor's got a reason, I think."

"And what's the matter with Eastbourne?" I asked.

"My dear man!" expostulated Prisms. "It's obvious you've never been there. It's a simply *appalling* place. The dullest, deadliest hole, crammed with the most *impossible* people."

"Yes, they are rather a weird crowd," assented Prunes. "We were there once, and I absolutely *loathed* it. You've got to be so beastly respectable all the time."

"And dress!" added Prisms. "Why, one day last year, I remember, the mater wore no less than three different costumes. That sort of thing may be all right in town; but when you're just bursting to get out, and you've got to wait for her, and then walk up and down the front and look proper, well— And on Sundays the guv'nor wears his topper!"

"Poor kid!" said the sympathetic Prunes.

"Now, at Whitsun," continued Prisms, "we went to Dawlish, and that was just gorgeous. Didn't wear stockings for a whole week, and had a ripping time. The right sort of people, you know, and we met some awfully jolly boys. Great fun they were. The mater had a donkey ride, too. A perfect scream. I'd like to go to Dawlish again. Think I'll sound the guv'nor about it."

She chewed the end of a plait meditatively and swung her lank, black legs about.

"What are your people doing this year?" she asked.

"Haven't the faintest idea," said Prunes. "They were talking of taking a place at Torquay, but I don't know if it's settled yet."

"Torquay! My holy aunt!" exclaimed Prisms. "Absolutely the *last* place, my dear."

"Oh, I shall be all right," said Prunes confidently. "You see, the mater's people, Aunt Beth and the boys, are going with us, and they're a real sporting crowd. And my people leave me alone pretty much."

"You're lucky," said Prisms. "Now, my guv'nor's folk—well, I can't stand 'em at all. They're all right, if you know what I mean, but—I don't know—there's a something— They're stuffy, you know.

"Last month I took Aunt Frances to that show at Olympia—the Tournament, isn't it?—and really, d'you know, she made me absolutely *squirm*. Asked the *attendants* the most *appalling* questions in a *frightfully* loud voice, and got so *absurdly* excited at everything. You'd have thought she'd just came up from the country. And she was wearing the *weirdest* hat! Black chip straw, trimmed with tartan ribbon and imitation grapes.

"I didn't enjoy the show one little bit. Kept wondering what on earth she was going to do next. We were sitting with some awfully toney people, too."

"It's all your own fault," I put in here. "You should have brought your aunt up properly."

"Oh, yes," said Prisms. "It's all very well for you. But you wouldn't like to take me out if I wore a hat trimmed with tartan and grapes, would you?"

"I should love it," I said.

"And you wouldn't like it if I talked in a loud voice, and said, 'Oh, do look at that poor man, he'll be killed'; and, 'Aren't the dear soldiers perfectly sweet'; and all that sort of thing, would you?"

"But you wouldn't," I said for want of a better answer. Long ago, I, too, was often put to the blush by such childish grown-ups.

"That's just it," said Prisms. "I shouldn't, but aunts do."

"One's people can make one feel awfully ridiculous at times," commented Prunes. "My pater, for instance. He's a dear old sort, of course, but he will talk shop when he's out with me. Asks me the French for everything we see. I think he does it to show off."

"Probably he's trying to find out if you are getting your money's worth at school," I suggested. That moved her to laughter.

"He doesn't know if it's right or not," she said. "I've tried it before now, and he never saw. P'raps he does it to improve his mind, poor dear."

"Have you ever heard of the Fifth Commandment?" I asked severely. Some delicate reproof, I felt, was needed.

"Oh, that!" said Prisms. " 'Honour thy pater,' isn't it? My dear man, that's nothing to do with it at all. Of course I honour my guv'nor and all that sort of thing. But fancy sticking in Eastbourne for a whole month."

"Besides," added Prunes, "it doesn't say anything about aunts, does it? I expect Moses had an aunt. Here's our station. By-bye."

"Tooraloo," I said.

75

Garden Magic

Peggy was in great trouble. Uncle Bungo had come for the weekend, and Mumsie had been obliged to go out, and dad wouldn't be home till late, and Podge was in next door swapping foreign stamps, and Binky Boy had gone to the vet's with distemper and hair falling out, and Uncle Bungo had come. He was there now, in the garden.

It was a dull and empty world, without form and void, and she was so glad to see me.

Uncle Bungo—Podge found the name in an atlas, and said it was a pity to waste it—Uncle Bungo was a stuffy person, and no fun at all.

Further (but I must not mention this to dad) he was an old chump.

He had been asleep in the garden all the afternoon, with his hands clasped across his watchchain, and a newspaper over his face.

"But you come and have a look at him," Peggy whispered. "He is funny, and he's ever so fast asleep."

I tiptoed over the gravel and beheld Uncle Bungo; a big, protuberant person; audibly sleeping; a blot on that fair garden.

The newspaper had slipped sideways, and his mouth was open. Peggy had all my sympathy.

Many men do not deserve the nieces they get, and this was one of them.

"I asked him to tell me a story," said Peggy, "and he said he was too busy. And I asked him what he was busy about, and he said finking. And I asked him what he was finking about, and he said, 'Run away and play.'

"And then I watched to see him fink, and he went to sleep. I s'pose he finks in his sleep."

She thought this over for a little while, then cuddled herself and giggled quietly.

"Free went in," she said half to herself, "and only one came out again. I 'specs two's gone right down."

"Two what?" I asked.

"Flies," said Peggy, and pointed to Uncle Bungo's sonorous mouth. "I watched two go in, and I fort if they didn't come out again I'd better wake him up. But I didn't, 'cos he'd only have been cross.

"Then another one went in, but that came out again, so I fort p'raps the others had come out and I hadn't seen them. But p'raps they didn't. They was only teeny ones." She clapped her feet together gleefully.

"And then there wasn't anyfing else to do, and I couldn't find Kershaw, and I was sorry all over till you came."

Kershaw, be it known, is a little person who lives in the top floor of a Canterbury Bell, and does wonderful things for Peggy and me. His name was originally Jack Anthus, and his sister Polly lived in the first-floor blossom.

But one night it rained and Jack's flat got full of water; so that Jack got a terrible cold, and sneezed and sneezed for days and days.

So, of course, he had to be called Kershaw, didn't he?

"I suppose Kershaw was frightened of Uncle Bungo," I said.

"P'raps 'at was it," mused Peggy. "And I'd fort of such a lovely plan. I was going to ask Kershaw to turn him into somefing."

"Well, maybe we can manage it without Kershaw this time," I said. "There's two of us, and I'm as big as Uncle Bungo. I'll learn him to be an uncle!"

"Oooo! Do let's," said Peggy, and cuddled herself again.

"All right," I said. "What shall it be?"

"Let's turn him into a—into a frog," suggested Peggy.

"A frog?" I said dubiously. "Well, of course, I could, but you see, there'd be such a lot over. Think of something else."

"Then turn him—turn him into a hip-pip—you know," said Peggy.

"A hip-hip-hooray," I suggested. "I don't think he's jolly enough for that. Only the very jolliest people can be hip-hip-hoorays."

"No, silly!" said Peggy. "You know what I mean. In the alfrebit book. H was a hip-pip-fing."

"You mean a hippopotamus," I said. "All right. There's just about enough of him for one of those. But you'll have to help." I carefully recited the Sloka used on such occasions, made the necessary passes, and it came off.

There he was!

Peggy clapped her hands and feet joyfully.

"Doesn't he look funny?" she said. "But s'posing he wakes up and finds out? Won't he be just wild!"

"Yes, I'd thought of that," I said, "and perhaps we'd better change him back. Besides, your father might come in any minute, and he'd be as cross as cross. Look how the deck chair's bending for one thing."

It was a bit of a job, but we managed it; and Uncle Bungo stirred a little in his sleep.

"Now something else," ordered Peggy excitedly. This was a great game.

"You must let me get my breath first," I remonstrated. "This sort of thing's wearing on a man. What would you like next?"

"Ooo! Anyfing," said Peggy. "Tell me some fings and I'll choose."

"Well, I can turn him into a giraffe," I said, "but then I should have to use one of his legs for the neck, and a giraffe with only one leg would look silly, wouldn't it? Besides being awkward about the house.

"Or I could turn him upside down, or into the middle of next week, or—"

"What's that like?" asked Peggy.

"The middle of next week," I explained, "is like a big square hole painted red, with nothing round it. Like the day before yesterday, only bigger."

"I don't think I'd like that," she said. "I know! Let's turn him into a steamroller."

" 'Fraid that'll want a bit of doing," I protested. "Now if Kershaw were here the two of us might manage it, but—anyway, I'll have a go." I took off my coat and moistened my palms.

Do you know, I tried and tried, and it simply would not come. Once or twice he really did begin to look like a steamroller, but he always slipped back just as the chimney stack was growing. Maybe I didn't get the words quite right.

So we gave that up, and tried some other things; and during the next half hour Uncle Bungo was by turns a pillar box, three Welsh rarebits (and there was such a lot of cheese over), a lawn mower, and a Swiss roll.

We were admiring this last when the bell rang.

"Oh, please do be quick," said Peggy, screwing up her hands. "That's Mumsie, and he'll wake up and she'll be so frightened. There's such a lot of him."

It was a tremendous effort, and the last little bit of roll vanished as Mumsie came into the garden, and Uncle Bungo woke up, looking rather tired. Peggy heaved a tremendous sigh of relief.

"That's all right," she said, "only there's a teeny-weeny bit of jam on his collar."

Under the Tape

An overcoat will cover a multitude of shiny patches, but one cannot wear an overcoat all summer, can one?

Mr. Sons, of Messrs. Creasey and Sons, sucked the point of his pencil, and looked at me slowly, beginning with my toes and rising inch by inch, more in sorrow than in anger, to my knees, my waist, my alleged chest, and my neck.

Once or twice on the way up he sighed. I told him not to do it.

"You make me feel as if I were trying to join the Army under false pretences," I said.

Mr. Sons sighed again, and wrinkled his forehead like a piece of tripe. As he reached for his book and tape measure he looked like a man smitten in years.

"A lounge, you said?" he remarked.

"Please, Mr. Sons," I answered. "Like the one I'm wearing."

"Like that?" he sighed.

"Like this," I said; "only new, of course."

"That sort of thing isn't much worn now," said Mr. Sons.

"This one is," I answered, and pointed out the places. Mr. Sons groaned and ate some more pencil.

"And please try to be bright about it," I added. "It's a lounge suit I want, not grave clothes."

He dropped to his knees, and I thought he said, "Alas!" or "Ah, me!"

Somehow, tailors always seem such despondent creatures. Maybe bad debts have something to do with it. Or perhaps their intimacy with the dimensions of their fellows breeds in them this profound melancholy.

Spring after spring they watch their customers' chests dwindling, or their waists swelling; until one year they are not; the new suitings attract them no more.

"Seventeen knee, sixteen ankle," sighed Mr. Sons, and looked up inquiringly. "They're being worn wider now," he added. "Eighteen seventeen."

But I was not to be shaken. "Same as these," I insisted.

"But they're old fashioned," protested Mr. Sons. "They're last year's."

"Well, and what if they are?" I retorted. "You needn't throw that up at me. For two pins I'll do the thing properly and grow side whiskers."

"But—" he began again, his voice quivering with emotion.

"Look here, Mr. Sons," I remonstrated. "Who's going to pay—I mean, who's going to wear the jolly things? Very well, then! Same as these." He flicked the tape measure round my chest; I took a deep breath and held it.

"When you've finished doing that," said Mr. Sons, "I'll measure you. You don't walk about like that, do you!"

Realising that I was getting red in the face I said I did not, and straightaway the chest collapsed. But I was a very Apollo for about three seconds.

"Thirty-three," said Mr. Sons in a hollow voice. "Thirty-three." He looked suspiciously at the place where I hope my left lung still lives and works.

"And what about it?" I asked. "What about thirty-three? Isn't it enough? Will it take up too much cloth? Can't you measure me for a suit without making insulting remarks?"

"I said thirty-three," sighed Mr. Sons. Then he turned up some back pages, and said, "It was thirty-four last time."

"Then your measure must be an old one," I said. "It's out of date, or else it's stretched. That inch there, for instance—number 5—that's a pretty long one, isn't it? By the way, how long do you give me to get my affairs in order?"

"Waist," said the tailor, and tickled me in the ribs. "Hold that there, please." He put one of my fingers on the end of the measure.

"Aren't you going to say you'll be round in a minute?" I asked. "My last tailor always did. It brightens the proceedings, you know. Creates a sort of friendly feeling. But then he was a bespoke tailor. Are you bespoke, Mr. Sons?"

"Thirty-seven," he answered, with a hush in his voice. "An increase, I think."

"Ah, then, that's the inch from my chest you've been making such a fuss about," I said. "It's slipped down. I knew it was somewhere about. What you lose on the swings you make up on the roundabouts, you know. Put on an inch, have I? And here are you, doing your best to belittle me, to make me out a miserable specimen of a forked radish; whereas I'm really rather a fine figure of a man—what!"

"You stoop more than you did," said Mr. Sons, "and your shoulder blades stick out."

"They're not shoulder blades," I pointed out. "They're rudimentary wings, Mr. Sons, and they're beginning to sprout. You'd better send in your bill."

After he had made me turn out my pockets and tickled me all over, about two and a half pages of the book were full of my lines of latitude and longitude.

"And now the style," said Mr. Sons.

"Same as this, please," I answered.

"Breast pocket outside," he said, and made a note. "That means longer lapels—sixteen, twenty, twenty-three."

"But I don't want a breast pocket outside," I said. "It isn't done. It's neither *de rigueur* nor *au fait* nor *comme il faut*. You see, I happen to know. All my friends—and I don't suppose you've been down Pall Mall since Dundreary's time."

"Thirteen and a half slack. S.B., slanting pockets, twenty-one, twenty-two, six buttons, low opening," said Mr. Sons, and wrote it all down.

"But—" I said.

"Lift your arm so," he directed.

I lifted it so, and said, "But look here—"

"Seven and a quarter, eight one," he read from the measure. "And you'd better have a high waist. Say about here."

"Don't tickle," I yelled; "and I won't have a waist. I hate a waist, 'specially a high one. On me, that is. And I won't have one, and if you write it in that book I'll stamp my feet and hold my breath, so there!"

"The young prince," said Mr. Sons solemnly, "the young prince wore a high-waisted lounge suit at the bazaar last week, and the Begum of Nepaul—"

"Not really!" I exclaimed. "The young prince! That alters the position, of course. Let me have two, Mr. Sons. The biggest you've got, and blow the expense." That reminded me of something.

"I suppose you couldn't—by the way, could you—look here, would you care to take these I've got on as part payment? It is done, I believe. Returned empties, don't they call 'em? No? Well, of course, you know your own business best, but I should have thought—the buttons and buttonholes are quite good, you know."

But he wouldn't hear of it.

I suppose I shall have another castor oil plant to look after presently.

The Wise Woman

After many a tough fight with the giant whose name is "I Don't Think," whose home is on the Hill of Derision, above the Valley of Doubt, little Ben Plimp has ceased to tell the story of his warts.

By the way, this Ben Plimp must not be confused with Ben Plimp, his father, who in the summer of '79 ate a three pound pot of home made strawberry jam in one afternoon for a bet; nor with Old Ben Plimp, his grandfather, who wore a red hollyhock in his coat at his third wife's funeral.

This Ben Plimp is famous for nothing but his warts, so far.

"D'you mean Old Ben or Ben?"

"No, Little Ben! Him with the warts."

They were trouble enough when he had them, but now they have gone—

Naturally, folk wanted to know all about it, and Little Ben had a frightful time. Everybody laughed, and nobody believed him, except, perhaps, Darky Silvester, and he was only convinced by a cut lip and the loss of an eye tooth.

"I've argued with 'em, an' I've swore oaths, an' I've walloped 'em, an' they only laughs. Three days' work I've lost over them warts. An' fights! Look at my knuckles! Besides the slate down to the Pipemakers' Arms that I broke over Jim Pleasants' head.

"But yet they won't believe me! An' so I've done with 'em, an' I'll never tell 'em no more about 'em, never, I won't."

Having first extracted from me a solemn promise to believe every word he was about to say, Little Ben consented to lay the facts before me. (He carries a fist that looks like a leg of mutton with knobs on it.)

"You see them?" said Little Ben, and held up his two hands. "Six months ago they was covered, they was. Covered so's I didn't know where to put 'em. A sight, they was!

"Got 'em, so they say, through a-washing of my hands in water what eggs'd been boiled in. I don't know about that, but I've had 'em ever since I was so high.

"Then my ole gran'fer, Old Ben Plimp, he says why didn't I go and see the Wise Woman down to Piper's Ghyll. A wunnerful woman she be by all accounts, and so I know now, for she took away my warts in the twinkling of an eye, as the saying is. After a week, there warn't a sign of 'em.

" 'Course, I'd heard of her, an' the things she done, but I dunno as I beleft all I heard. Such tales they do tell. There was Susie Pett's kid as had one eye all atwist an' not looking same way's t'other. An' the Wise Woman give her a lotion to rub on it, an' though it ain't what you might call all right now, it's made a sight o' difference, so Susie Pett do say.

"Then there was young Reuben Oakey as married my woman's cousin over to Mockbeggar. He go to her reg'lar for bottles of stuff for pimples, yerbs an' things, an' a power o' good they've done him, too, so he do say.

"Not that I set much store by all them tales, but the doctor never done me no good except burn my hands, so gran'fer he says why didn't I go over and tell the Wise Woman about it. An' so I did.

"Not as I beleft all I'd heard about her, mind; but just to see if there was anything in it.

"She's a rum ole woman, an' lives in a rum ole house thatched with bracken, an' believe me, she could hold a penny 'twixt her nose and chin, an' her face it be all screwed up an' brown like a medlar.

"Well, I knocks on the door an' goes inside. 'Twas same as any other cottage, with bundles of green stuff hung up to dry in the chimbley.

"An' the old woman, she say: ' 'Tis young Ben Plimp,' she say, 'An' he have come about his warts,' she say."

Little Ben leaned forward and pushed his face very close to mine.

" 'He have come about his warts,' she say. What d'you think of that, mister?"

"Wonderful," I agreed. "Who could have told her?"

"Not me," said Ben. "I hadn't never been nigh nor by the cottage till then. I reckon she just about knew somehow.

"Well, I never said a word, being a bit took aback like. An' she looks at me cunning, an' she say, 'Come you again tomorrow night after sunset by yourself, an' bring you three pieces of silver, big 'uns, an' tell no one.'

" 'Half-crowns?' I says.

" 'Bigger,' says she.

" 'Four shillin's?' I says.

" 'They'm out o' date an' dead,' says she.

" 'Five shillin's?' I says.

" 'Three five shillin's will do,' she says; 'An' let them be bright an' shining an' new.'

"I tell you, I had a sight o' trouble getting those three crown-pieces, but get 'em I did; two King Edwards an' one King Jarge. An' the Edward warn't so shiny as t'other, so I polished 'em up with brick dust an' paraffin, an' next night I goes over to the old woman's again.

"She was waiting for me, an' it was creepy in that cottage. 'Twas dimpsey outside, but inside 'twas blind man's holiday, with one candle an' a bit o' fire that went up an' down, an' gert big shadows running all over the wall an' across the ceiling.

"There was some mutton broth stewing on the hob, an' that smelt good an' comfortable of onions, so I wasn't exactly afraid.

"She never said nothing, but took the fifteen shillin's, an' looked at 'em close to the candle. Then she got a little pot an' put 'em in, an' poured in something out of a bottle, an' set it over the fire. By an' bye it begins to bubble, an' she stirs it, an' sprinkles something on the fire, so it all burns blue, an' she looks like a ghost.

"Then she puts something else on, an' it all burns red, an' she stirs it again, an' sings some poetry into it, but I've forgot what that was."

"I think I know the song," I said, and Little Ben stared. "Wasn't it—

'Wart, wart, long and short,
  Go and shrivel up to nought?' "

"That was it," said Little Ben; "that was it, only you ain't got the toon just right. How did you know?"

"I heard some youngsters singing it," I answered, "only their tune was 'Fool, fool, come to school.' "

"The blarmed young varmints," said Mr. Plimp. "Let me catch one of 'em at it. I'll learn 'em.

"Well, presently the ole gal she looks to the pot, an' says it's done. An' she pours out the liquor, all dark blue it was, an' puts it in a bottle, an' corks it up.

" 'That's valuable,' she says, 'so don't waste it, for it's silver broth, an' your money's all boiled away.' That was a bit of a setback that I hadn't reckoned on, but I didn't say nothing. An' I pays her a shillin' for the stuff. Thinks I, if it'll do away with my warts 'tis money well spent.

"An' so 'twas, too. Morning an' night, as she told me, I rubbed it in till I was that sore—but they went away." He looked at the backs of his hands closely. "Wunnerful, I call it, an' if that there Jim Pleasants has any more to say about it—

"I asks you, mister, as man to man, have they gone?"

I said they had, but they hadn't, not all of them.

"There you are, then," said Mr. Plimp triumphantly. "There they was, an' there they ain't, an' don't that prove it?"

I thought of Darky Silvester's cut lip, and of Mr. Pleasants' broken sconce, and I said it did. But when Mr. Plimp had gone home, I scooped a little hole in the ground and in accordance with ancient tradition I whispered into it, "I don't think."

Then I felt better.

Two on a Tour

The pink *mousseline de sole*—that flimsy stuff with dots on it—at Messrs. Vanity's has gone up. Whereas in June, 1913, it cost one-and-eleven-three, last week it had risen to two-and-a-penny-three.

So much Charlotte told me as she stepped on my feet and hit me in the face with a china jar of potted ham and tongue. She added that it (the increase in the price of the *m. de s.*) was due, she had heard, to some war somewhere or other, and she thought it was grossly unfair.

By this time she had stopped falling about, finding safe anchorage in the seat next to me. Catherine followed, and sat in Charlotte's lap while the bus took a corner. After that she moved up one.

Let me hasten to explain that neither of these ladies is anything at all to me. I was awfully glad to be in the same bus with them, of course, otherwise I should never have heard about Marjorie's fiancé or Robert's complexion.

The former is an electrical engineer; the latter is mostly blotches, and Robert has tried simply everything. At present he is hard at work with lemon juice and massage, but so far there is little improvement.

Life can be very hard.

When I wish to talk in a bus, I do so in tense whispers; with an eye on the man opposite, who always looks as if he were trying to look as if he were not listening.

Not so Charlotte and Catherine. They told all of us all about it; the clergyman near the door who read the advertisements on the roof until the back of his neck gave out; the pink young soldier who looked as if he had been melted down and poured into his uniform; the girl with the bundle of trousers over her arm, and myself. And I expect the driver must have heard bits here and there.

When they had arranged themselves, "Look here, my dear," said Charlotte; "you change places with me. You'll be more comfortable here."

"No, no," said Catherine, "you stay where you are. I'm quite all right."

"But I insist," said Charlotte. So they changed places. I think Charlotte scored. There was a note of satisfaction in her "That's better!"

Suddenly, remembering something she had left unfinished at Sevenoaks or Nine Elms, wherever they started it, Charlotte picked up the broken thread.

"As I pointed out, there's no need whatever for them to know such people. They ought to consider Herbert's future. And what do you think Helen said? She said—" and the rest was breathed close into Catherine's ear, where it must have tickled horribly.

This was agony for the rest of us, and the girl with the trousers over her arm actually leaned forward a little. But I don't think she got it.

"There, now!" said Catherine, with a deep breath.

Charlotte continued: "I said to her, 'Well, as you've made your bed so you must lie on it.' "

"Fares, please," said the conductor.

"Oh, the fares," said Charlotte. "How much is it? Oh, conductor, does this bus go to Oxford Circus? You're sure? Very well, then. Two to Oxford Circus." She opened a handbag and offered him a potash lozenge.

"I'll pay," said Catherine.

"No," said Charlotte. "I've got some coppers."

"But I've got plenty," said Catherine.

"So have I, and I want to get rid of them," said Charlotte.

"But you paid coming up," said Catherine.

"Never mind," said Charlotte. "I want to get rid of these coppers. I'm sure I've got some somewhere."

"But I insist," said Catherine, and dropped a vanity case.

"That's quite all right," said Charlotte. "I've got—" and she stooped after a scent bottle.

Then Catherine emptied her bag into her lap, and I retrieved a tape measure and a cachou. "You really must let me pay," she said. "I've got heaps of coppers somewhere."

"Fares, please!" said the conductor.

"My dear Catherine," began Charlotte, and "My dear Charlotte," began Catherine; and both commenced to rummage again.

"I really wish you'd let me pay," said Catherine.

"Nonsense," said Charlotte. "I'll pay. I've got a lot of coppers to get rid of. They're so heavy, and—"

"Fares, please!" said the conductor.

"Where are they? I had a lot when I left home. Oh, of course, I bought some chocolate, didn't I?"

"Then you must let me pay," said Catherine.

"No, indeed," said Charlotte. "I'm taking you out, and I insist upon paying. Tuppence, isn't it?" she asked the conductor. Then gave him a two-shilling piece. "Have you change? Two to Oxford Circus. I thought I had a lot of coppers."

" I wish you had let me pay," said Catherine, still rummaging.

"Not at all!" said Charlotte. Then she had a bright thought. "I'll tell you what, dear. You shall pay for the tea."

I think Charlotte scored again there.

For a while both busied themselves in packing their little bags and dropping smelling salts and pearl buttons and nail scissors, and picking them up again.

Then Charlotte looked through the bus window.

"I suppose this bus does go to Oxford Circus?" she asked, and looked suspiciously at the conductor. Several of us assured her that it did.

"I expect it's all right," said Catherine. "Most of them do."

"And as I said to Arthur only yesterday," pursued Charlotte, "it isn't as if the poor girl had done anything. It was entirely her mother's fault, and I shall speak to her most strongly about it. Why, do you know—" and she blew the rest into Catherine's ear again.

"I'm not in the least surprised," said Catherine.

"Anyway, I hope I shall be able to get some more of that figured cretonne," said Charlotte. "I've got a piece of string here just the length I want. It's for a footstool, you know. We haven't passed Oxford Circus yet, have we? Conductor! Conductor! You'll let us know when we get to Oxford Circus, won't you?"

He punched a ticket with unnecessary ferocity and said he would.

"I told him to try glycerine and cucumber," Charlotte went on. "And if that doesn't do any good, I think he ought to see a specialist. And he's quite a nice looking boy, ordinarily. Such a pity. I think it must be his blood."

"I've heard eau de Cologne spoken very well of," said Catherine. "I believe actresses use it. And milk, too. Baths of milk."

"Oxford Circus!" called the conductor.

"And he's going up for the Army next year," said Charlotte.

"Oxford Circus," repeated the conductor.

"Oh, here we are!" said Catherine, and they both upheaved.

"I suppose you don't go past Vanity's?" asked Charlotte. "It's only a little way further down."

"Not with these tickets, ma'am," said the conductor. "Another penny."

"Oh, I don't think that's fair at all," commented Charlotte. "It's not more than five minutes' walk. Let's see, did I have an umbrella? No, I don't think so. Yes, I did. Oh, no! Of course, I remember. Arthur said the glass was going up, so I put it back. But I thought I'd be on the safe side, so I put on my black voile. That cashmere does spot so."

Long after they were out of sight we could still hear Charlotte.

A Presentation

For nearly an hour Jellicoe had walked by my side, muttering broken phrases to himself, isolated words, fragments of what sounded like a political peroration, mixed up with occasional expressions, uttered through the teeth, that were anything but parliamentary. Also, his usually alabaster brow was ruled with lines, so that one might have written a waltz on it.

Once or twice I drew his attention to the beauties of our walk, but he only gibbered and made mouths at me.

"See," I would say, "yonder chimney pot, or hay stack, or duck pond (as the case might be), how wonderfully it takes the light. Observe the beauties of this gnarled thorn or that gasometer."

From under his breath came answer: "Unaccustomed as I am ... auspicious occasion ... noteworthy occasion ... melancholy occasion ... impossible to overrate ... underrate ... overrate ... oh, bust it!"

"When you feel it coming on again—" I began.

But he only murmured: "Far be it from me ... far be it ... far be it ... shut up, you silly chump."

At the end of another two miles he stopped, climbed on a gate, and unbosomed himself.

"The fatheads at the office," he said, "are getting up a presentation to one of the staff, and I've got to do it; and I've never made a speech in my life, and the boss will be there, and all the heads, and—and I wish I was dead."

"Why ever didn't you say so before?" I said. "Presentations are my strong suit. I've stood in the background at many a one, watching presenter and presentee perspiring. I'll help you, of course, if you'll tell me all about it. What are you presenting?"

"That's not decided yet," said Jellicoe. "They've only just thought of it. What's the usual?"

"Depends largely on the circumstances," I said. "In the case of an ordinary wedding a clock is the correct thing. Contrariwise, if it's a golden wedding they usually present the victim with a clock, while for long service or long distance records, one generally gives a clock.

"Twenty years service, a clock; twenty-five years, a clock; thirty years, a timepiece. Why, I know a man who's been fifty years in one situation, been married twice, and used to be a good sprinter. He's got his house furnished with clocks. Had to retire because he couldn't keep them wound, and when they strike twelve—"

"I suppose we ought to give him a clock, then," said Jellicoe.

"Unless you want to strike out a new line," I said. "People with no respect for the conventions have been known to give such absurd things as toast racks or rose bowls. But with a clock there can be no mistake.

"There it will stand on the mantelpiece, ticking blithely away, to show the recipient that life is short and time is fleeting; tick-ticking like little undertakers' hammers, every tick a nail. Very grateful and comforting. Who is the lucky man?"

"It's old Barnacles, our cashier," said Jellicoe. "He's only a young man, and he's leaving us to take up a better job. That's different from your example, isn't it?"

"Ah, then, in that case," I said, "you'd better give him a clock. By the way, is this Barnacles person beloved of all who know him?"

"Oh, crumbs!" said Jellicoe, from which I gathered that the answer was in the negative. "Beloved of all— Look here, I wish you'd take this seriously. If you can't help don't hinder."

I assured him that I was in deadly earnest and went on helping him.

"Having decided on the nature of the gift—you'd better jot down the word 'clock' on your cuff; you might forget it—the next thing is the speech. That's where you shine. Got a piece of paper? Right! Now, then, how about the opening?"

"I'd thought of 'Unaccustomed as I am,' " said Jellicoe nervously.

"I know you had," I answered. "You always do. But this time we'll try something original. First you must find a suitable form of address. 'Dearly beloved,' or 'Kind friends,' or 'Ladies and gentlemen,' or 'Men and fellow workers.' "

"I've thought that out," said Jellicoe. "I shall start, 'Mr. Barnacles and gentlemen.' "

"So that's settled," I went on, "and the rest is easy. 'Mr. Barnacles and gentlemen. We are gathered here this afternoon to—er—you know what I mean, and it gives me the greatest pleasure (or pain, as the case may be) to—er bear witness to—er the greatest esteem—' By the way, you haven't much use for this Barnacle person, have you?"

"Oh, crumbs!" said Jellicoe again.

I continued: " '—the tremendous and unbounded esteem and—er regard which we have for our whilom, or quandom, or erstwhile colleague.

" 'As the dispenser of our salaries (better pause there till the hooting subsides), we feel it incumbent (make a note of that) on us to mark our—er—' You see what I'm getting at—and—well, I don't quite see how it goes now, but, then, I don't know Barnacles. Most likely the applause will help you out there."

"Thanks, awfully," said Jellicoe.

"Next," I continued, "we come to the actual presentation. This must be done very carefully.

"At the first mention of the gift, turn your eyes to the clock or timepiece, as the case may be, and stare fixedly at that, twiddling your watch chain with your left hand, thus.

" 'Therefore, gentlemen, we have decided that our old and crusted friend Barnacles should not leave us without some mark, etc., etc., and to that end we wish to—er present him with this—er handsome clock.' At this point you pick up the clock in your left hand, and hold it at arm's length. By the way, have you got any dumbbells?

"The rest is simple. 'Inadequate as is our little gift to show a tithe of the admiration we feel for the sterling qualities of the dear departing, yet he knows—' and there you'd better work in a bit of poetry or Shakespeare or Something. Gives a tone to the proceedings.

"I suggest ' 'Tis not in mortals to command success,' or 'It stopped short, never to go again.' Round things off nicely."

"I see," said Jellicoe, looking over his notes; "but I wanted to mention 'this auspicious occasion.' "

"I shouldn't do that if I were you," I said. "Better leave the guv'nor something, and he's sure to like that. Then Barnacles will have to say a few words in a voice broken with emotion; somebody proposes a vote of thanks to you, and somebody else seconds that; and you reply, and they reply, and the guv'nor says a few words, in the middle of which the clock will strike twelve very slowly and solemnly.

"That gives the boss a chance to say something about 'this striking timepiece' (loud laughter). Oh yes, he will. And that's about all, I think.

"Barnacles will say something about the happiest hours of his life, and the home of his childhood, and friends that stick closer than a brother (here the clock will strike twelve again).

"There are a lot more votes of thanks and thanks for votes of thanks, and replies to votes of thanks, and secondings and carryings of votes of thanks. Then you all wipe your clammy hands in your handkerchiefs, and Barnacles will put the clock in his hat (whereupon it will strike twelve), and take the firm round the corner to quench its thirst. If the clock came to £3 10s. the thirst usually comes to £3 14s. 9d., so you get your money back all right."

A Pathetic Pen

As the last faint bars of the "Unfinished" drifted through the trees, the man at the other end of the seat sighed heavily and looked at me. That I saw with the tail of my eye, and so stuck steadily to my book.

He wanted to talk, I thought, while I wanted to read; and the book would not permit of interruption. He edged a little nearer. Certainly he was going to talk, but I would pretend not to hear.

Dreadful thought! He might ask me for a match. Even a deaf man would have to hear that. I read doggedly on, not seeing what I read, and—

"Could you oblige me with a light?" he asked.

I shut the book with a bang, and handed him the box.

"A beautiful evening," he went on. " 'The glorious deathbed of a glorious day,' as Tennyson so beautifully says."

"Does he?" I asked.

"I think you will find it in 'Comus,' " he answered.

"Shall I?" I questioned.

"A superb evening, but melancholy," he pursued. "Even as the day is dying, so the year is fading to winter."

A scorched leaf floated down from a plane tree, and a sparrow dropped to investigate. The man crept three inches nearer.

"A week ago," he sighed, "I was in these gardens. They closed then at nine o'clock. The board now says 8.45."

"Alas!" I answered. He seemed so miserable about it that I offered him another match.

"Next week," he continued, "it will be 8.30."

"And it only wants about five months to Christmas," I added, and sighed like a furnace, or as near like one as I could manage.

He was a doleful, seedy person. His hat was a shocking hat, and his chin—either he was trying to grow a beard or else he was trying not to. Whichever it was, he had only just begun.

Apart from these things, he annoyed me in other ways. He annoyed me because I could not read his riddle. Was it a night's lodging, or a meal, or a bus fare, that I should presently be asked to lend him? Ignoble thoughts, but then you should have seen his hat and whiskers.

He returned to the subject of the falling leaf and fading flower.

"From seedtime to harvest, from harvest to seedtime—look here, mister, d'you want to buy a good fountain pen cheap?"

"Hooray!" I cried, immensely relieved. "Thank you, thank you, for those kind words. I had a suspicion that I was misjudging you."

He stared for a second, then took a packet from his coat.

"It's a good pen," he said. "A real Swan and Edgar. Vulcanite reservoir, self filling, centrifugal pump action, and 18-carat gold feed. Heigho! I wish I'd got all the cheques it has signed. That pen has been a real friend to me." He dashed a tear from one of his eyes as I took the pen from him.

"It looks a bit off its gold feed now," I remarked. "But I am a little disappointed. I rather expected it would be a tie pin."

"I've got a tie pin, if you want one," he said quickly. "A beauty! First water, and hardly chipped. It's been a real friend to me has that tie pin. We've seen the world together. And I've got a pair of gold links, and a solitaire ring, and a Russia leather cigar case with gold corners. Been a good friend to me, that solitaire ring has. The nights we've had! As Euripides says in his what's-its-name—you remember the passage?"

"Perfectly," I answered. "Good old Euripides! But I'm afraid I don't quite understand. Are not these things the proceeds of a burglary? Were you not going to whisper to me, with nods and becks and wreathed smiles, as your Mr. Tennyson so finely puts it, that these articles were 'crook'? Got on the cross? Dirt cheap because the what-d'you-call-'ems were after you—the narks, or is it the lags?"

The seedy man laughed quietly.

"No, I wasn't going to do anything of the sort," he said. "Not to you. That'd be too risky with you. You'd threaten to call the police. And I hate scenes.

"When I saw you sitting here, reading poetry, and looking at the sunset like a sick calf, I said to myself it's got to be pathos.

"I was going to be a broken down gent, parting with the last links—solid gold links—between me and my prosperous days. It would have been a lovely story—how I had lived a life of sumptuous ease, wearing evening dress all day, dining at the Savoy, motor car, Ascot, box at the Opera—all lost at cards, curse them! A splendid story! I should have enjoyed it."

I apologised for having spoilt the lie, and the fallen one continued.

"I was undecided between that and the broken down journalist. Fleet Street isn't so far away, is it? And many's the stirring clarion call I've blown on this fountain pen with the pump action and the 18-carat feed. Then drink started its dreadful work. Ah, me!

"As a matter of fact, between me and you and the gatepost, I simply *can't* drink. I get ill long before I get drunk.

"You see, you had me in a corner. The way you snapped at me I could see there was something wrong with my bit of Tennyson. That put me off, else I'd thought of one of the Varsities. Cambridge for pref. I've been an old Cambridge man several times, and I got rid of seventeen fountain pens at Oxford only last month."

"Well, you're an enterprising scoundrel, anyway," I said, and he lifted his shocking bad hat with a grin. "But you must make a lot of mistakes."

"Heaps!" he answered. "Heaps! Why, last Sunday in Hyde Park I paid a penny for a chair in the band enclosure, and sat next to such a dear old gent. Long hair, soft hat, gold-headed cane. They were playing something dismal and quiet, and in the middle of it I broke down and sobbed like a child. Now that wants doing. But the old gent let me cry and cry till there wasn't a drop of moisture left in me. Then he asked me if I was sad because I hadn't sold my tie pin. You know, that sort of thing is horribly discouraging.

"Hallo! They're shutting up. Look here, mister; before you go, you have a look at that fountain pen. It's real good stuff, for all I've been telling you, and dirt cheap. A real Edison and Swan."

"I'm afraid not," I said. "You see, the nib is just copper and the feed is a fake and the pump business doesn't pump; and, besides, it isn't even stolen property."

"I wish you wouldn't change your mind so often," said the pen merchant. "I don't know what to do. But if you want a 'crook' pen, then this is it. Part proceeds of a burglary."

"In which case," I said, "I am afraid I mustn't touch it. As Demosthenes says—you remember the passage?"

"Perfectly," said the seedy one. "But it doesn't apply. Now don't go away. Don't leave your old college chum. I've got to get rid of this pen before I can get a dinner, and I'd like you to have it for old time's sake. But if your conscience worries you, I may as well tell you that I picked it up about half an hour ago, near the bandstand, and I'll take a bob for it."

"Then you haven't a stock of them on you?" I asked. "And you don't go round sobbing and sighing and telling pathetic stories of your luscious past?"

"Never had a fountain pen before in my life," he said. "Nor a past. But, you see, you thought yourself so blooming clever I hadn't the heart to disappoint you. Besides which, I'm such a natural born liar that I can't believe a word I say.

"Shall we call it a bob, mister? I'm that hungry, you don't know. A little bob ... That's all right! I've got change ... Seven-and-six, eight, nine shillings. There you are, and thank you very much. Well, I must be toddling. Don't the days draw in!"

·

The Arrival

As the 4.23 grunted up the incline I heard the distant rustle of the tide in the bay, a sound for which I had waited, so it seemed, for years. There was one other man in the carriage, and he knelt on the seat and clapped his hands unashamedly.

"You'll find it all just about as you left it last year," said the stationmaster through a mouthful of bass. He had left his carnations to take my ticket. "Just about as you left it, barring some new pups up to the 'Lodestar.' I be going down to see them tomorrow, or maybe Sunday. Good pups they be, so I hear … Did I get your ticket? Ah, yes, here she be. Just a minute while I get my glasses … Now, then!"

He read the ticket slowly from top to bottom, nodding approval here and there; then, remarking that he hoped it was all right, he opened the gate and released me.

I waited, admiring his garden, while he sent the little train about its business, put the signal at danger, shunted a goods truck, shooed a cat off the line, opened the level crossing gates, and read the labels on four dead rabbits that lay on the platform.

"Just about as you left it," he repeated when he had finished these things. "Let's see, did I get your ticket? Ah, yes, of course. Well, I hope you'll have a nice time, but it do look powerful like rain. Still, we can't grumble. Had a fine summer if we don't get any more." He brushed a wasp from his brow and turned to his garden.

"Trunk?" he repeated after me. "Trunk? Oh, you do mean that great green box. Yes, she'm gone up to the house. My, but she was a powerful heavy box, and difficult to handle. Nigh broke our hearts getting her out of the van, she did. Dunno when I've had such a struggle with a box. But you'll find her up there all right, and not a mark on her. 'Course, we handled her careful, knowing she was yours, but as I says to George, our new porter, 'George,' I says, 'he'm all of half a ton, and might be full of iron.'

" 'Granite, I reckon,' says George. But we got her out, and—" (one shilling) "—thank you, sir. Not but what we earnt it, for she were that heavy—but p'raps you'll be seeing George yourself?" He put some more bass in his mouth, and went back to the garden.

Down the narrow path I went singing, while in the illimitable blue above a mewing gull hung poised. At the top of the blackberry hedge pink fingers of honeysuckle waved, and as I fished for the stalk with my stick, George came along.

"Morning, sir; afternoon, I mean," said George. "Be you stopping long? Ah, then, that'll be your box as I carried out o' the truck yesterday. A gert green thing 'twas, as big as a 'ouse. Lord, but 'er did give us socks in a manner o' speaking. I says to stationmaster, I says, ' 'Er be full of granite, I should reckon,' I says.

"And then, getting 'er on to the truck, she slipped, she did, an' smashed my toes all to jelly. Well, pretty nigh! But we got her up, with a push an' a haul an' a shove, an' down the lane to Sam Trevagissey's cart, an' I all but put my shoulder out hoistin' 'er in.

"A brute to handle, she was, an' I do ache all over like I'd been walloped with a stick. 'Alf a ton if she weighed an ounce—" (one shilling) "—much obliged, I'm sure. Then you'll be seein' Sam yourself?"

Over the little footbridge I went, waving my stick because I was alive, and the trunk had arrived, and the sky was blue, and the sea just the darker sediment of the sky. Across the quivering heat of the bay the purple cliff rose, crowned by the shafts of the worked out tin mines. Crows live there now, and, at even when the magic light comes up out of the sea, these are the battlemented towers of fabric, which none should pass without their fingers crossed, or cold iron in their pockets.

Along the line of black weed that marks high water, walked Sam Trevagissey, just as he walked last year. Nothing changed about him, except—surely last year he wore two gold earrings, where now he sports but one?

I picked up that story later. Some trouble about his share in a catch of fish, and (so the boy said) a glorious fight. Since when Sam walks the shore looking for his jewelled lobe.

As soon as he saw me his hand went to the small of his back, where one keeps lumbago, and his eyes screwed up in agony. But I forestalled him.

"Sam," I said, "is the pony still alive?"

"Only just," said Sam. "Gets over me why, when peoples comes on a holiday, they must bring all they got with 'em. All last night my old woman was a-rubbin' me with horse oils, and 's'mornin' she's tendin' the pony. Black and blue, I be, and the pony all of a muck sweat with lather.

"Dang it! but she was just about a ton I should reckon; an' that last bit up Lamp Post Hill broke 'er poor heart, so it did. A good pony, she were. An' the cart, too! All lopsided it be with the weight of it. Dunno but what she'll be much use anymore—" (two shillings) "— still, I've 'ad worse, an' you'll find 'er all right, with never a dent in 'er anywheres. 'Ad to get young 'Arry Bryant an' two-three of the boys to give us a shove, but I s'pose you'll be seein' them sep'rit, maybe?

" 'Twas a main 'ard struggle, but we done it, the pony an' me an' the boys ... Nice an' fine now, bain't it? But I don't some'ow think it'll last. Wind's gettin' round into the west quarter, an' the gulls ain't settled all day. An' now I'll be gettin' up-along for some more of that elephant's embrocation stuff. Ouch!"

From behind the hills, all pink in the light of the falling sun, the moon uprose, a silver sickle set in blue, and from the safe harbour of the rock pools came the shrill cries of paddling youngsters.

Master Harry Bryant and his three friends were sitting on the doorstep waiting for me; and—

"I shoved 'er, mister," said Harry, and "I hiked her out," said another, and "We got her up the hill," added the other two, and "She worn't half heavy," they all chanted together.

"Coming up the slope," said one, "she'd have slipped off an' gone down to the bottom if I hadn't put my foot behind the wheel—" (threepence each) "—nigh smashed all my toes up, that did. Hc limped up and down to show me how he would never again be able to work for his living.

Little Billy Polden, my landlord's eight year old son, was sliding down the stairs when I went inside, but seeing me he stopped to suck his finger. That, I learned, had been sadly nipped under the lid of the trunk. No, he wasn't helping. Only trying to get it open! I gave him a cigarette picture, and he went on sliding downstairs.

But you should have heard his father!

Called Up

Here, where our only excitements are bathing and blackberrying, with an occasional fresh litter of pups to be sorted into sheep and goats, the news came through to us slowly.

The roar and drag of the tide under our windows woke us and lulled us to sleep as usual, the glad days were full of blue sky and languor; and on the wind from the hills behind came the clatter of reaping machines marshalling the yellow wheat into orderly stooks.

Not until the morning of the third day did we fully grasp all that it might mean.

At no time was there panic; no war fever took hold of us. Here and there maybe a wild rash broke out. For instance, cream went up threepence the pound, and two mornings running I was a rasher short at breakfast. Miss Poldew, our postmistress, too, got a little mixed, and refused to take gold coin of the realm. She knew, she said, that there was something about gold in the papers; either that she should not take it or that she should. So to be on the safe side she trusted me with some stamps until headquarters made the matter clear.

Since Barley's Great Dramatic and Variety entertainment visited us a month ago ("Maria Martin" and "The Burglar's Baby" for twopence) breakfast has always been set to the tune of "Violets," which the lady who played Maria used to sing (with her hair down) in the interval.

On Tuesday the ritual was missing, and it was a quiet and doleful Miriam who inquired how many lumps. Her thirteen years seemed to sit heavily on her shoulders, and there was a lack of vivacity about her bare legs when she came down the garden.

"Anything the matter?" I asked. "Burnt the bacon or boiled the eggs too hard?"

"Pooh!" said Miriam, "that wouldn't worry me. It's this war I'm thinking about, not your silly old breakfast."

"Is there any news then?" I asked.

"News!" said Miriam contemptuously. "While you're snoring away upstairs—but there, you wouldn't wake up if the old Germans came marching up the coombe, you wouldn't. There's five chaps gone from the village, and—and—my—my—my Ern's been called up." Her nether lip trembled.

"Your Ern?" I asked. "Didn't know you'd got an Ern. What is he? Territorial? Reservist? Where's he gone? Who is he?"

"My Ern," she said proudly, quite collected now. "My boy, Young Ern Dewey. We'm engaged."

I laid my knife down. "Engaged?" I gasped. "Miriam, does your father know of this?"

"Partly," said Miriam. "He knows we'm walking out together. What about it?"

"And is Mr. Dewey in the Territorials?" I asked.

"He's not old enough yet," she said. "He's a Scout. And he's been called up. Been in the Scouts two years now, and he's got badges for heaps of things. Carpentering and breadmaking and first aid and all sorts."

"Oh, a Scout," I said, a little relieved. "A Boy Sprout."

Miriam stood up, flaming. "That's right! Be funny," she barked. "Think it clever, don't you!" (I didn't.) "Might be glad of him some day."

"I'm glad of him now," I said. "Jolly glad. And I wish I could do carpentry and first aid. I'm sorry, but it slipped out. We thought they were funny once, you know. But they're fine. And where has your Ern gone?"

"He's away down along by Petling's Farm, looking after a level crossing," said Miriam.

"Then shall we go down together and see him doing it?" I asked, and Miriam dashed at the breakfast things.

Sure enough, there was the level crossing and there was the Scout doing sentry-go across the rails. Miriam giggled excitedly.

"Don't he look a treat!" she said; then called him. "Er-ern! Ooo-oy, Er-ern!"

But the sentry marched stolidly on.

"Er-ern! That's him. Wish he'd come and talk to us … Er-ern!"

The Scout came towards us, his staff at the "ready."

"Orders to hold no communication with civilians," he said, and stared blankly at Miriam.

"Coo!" said that young lady. "What you swanking about? Who wants to talk to you? Look after your silly old railway by yourself, then." And she turned and pulled me away.

"He's all right, though, ain't he?" she said presently. "Looks proper. I cleaned up all his buttons last night. He'll look after it all right. They won't get past him."

"He's fine!" I said. "The way he wouldn't talk to you was magnificent. But all the same, you know, the Kaiser—"

"Oh, *him!*" snorted Miriam.

Time-Expired

Some two years ago Mr. Peter Butcher sold me a pup, a nice little fox terrier, with that black roof to his mouth which, I understand, is the hallmark of the thoroughbred.

His favourite diet consists of slippers and cats, on which he thrives amazingly. I have never actually caught him eating a cat, but I have frequently found him in the middle of my violas, coughing over a mouthful of fur. And as to slippers—!

On the strength of this business transaction, Mr. Butcher has since cultivated my further acquaintance. He is a fine figure of a man; tall, and thickly built, with eyes that meet yours frankly, and a moustache like a stage brigand. A week ago you might have seen him standing outside the Lincoln Green Picturedrome, dressed in a pale blue uniform with gold epaulettes, shouting and flogging his leg with a swagger cane, and altogether looking and behaving very like an emperor.

Tonight there is another man to entice people into the picturedrome, and his efforts to fill out Mr. Butcher's uniform are a source of endless delight to the youth of the neighbourhood.

Ten days ago I stood admiring Mr. Butcher as he strutted up and down the pavement, when he beckoned to me.

"Evening, guv'nor," he said. " 'Ow's the dorg? (Now showin'! Now showin'!) Don't go away. I want to 'ave a chat with you. (A new an' thrillin' drama, entitled 'The Murderer's Mother.') Been looking for you these three nights. (Continuous performance. Plenty of seats.) 'Alf a minute an' I'm goin' to 'ave a breather. (Tuppence, fourpence, and sixpence. Superb ventilation.) We'll pop across the road to the Baker's Arms. (No waitin'. Now showin'! 'Oppit, you kiddies. Time you was in bed.) I've got a throat on me like a desert island. An' I partic'larly want to 'ave a chow with you … Ah, the lights is down. Come on!"

And I trotted alongside the stately blue personage to the Baker's Arms. In three seconds Mr. Butcher was wiping his moustache and clucking with satisfied desire.

"Can't talk 'ere," he said; "besides which I ain't got time. Could you give me a look up tonight? I'm off duty at nine, an' I want your advice. You know where I 'ang out? Right you are, guv'nor. So long then, for the present."

I knew Mr. Butcher's address because on several occasions Gelert, the fox terrier, has had attacks of nostalgia, and I have had to fetch him back.

The pale blue uniform being the property of the picture palace had been left behind, and that night the emperor was dressed in the trousers and shirt of a man who has done his day's work.

"Come upstairs," said Mr. Butcher, and led the way. "And now we'll lock the door to keep out the nosey parkers." He sat down and sucked awhile at his pipe.

"I'm fed up with all this," he said, presently. "Fed up! 'Now showin', now showin'.' An' me six foot one with a forty-three chest. 'Taint a job I'm proud of, an' I'm goin' to chuck it … 'Ow old d'you reckon I am? No kid. Straightology! 'Ow old?"

I hazarded forty.

"That's something towards it," he said. "I'm forty-four. You say forty, an' if I 'ad a shave—that'd make a diff, wouldn't it? And I've looked after myself, too! Look at that." He stripped his shirt to the waist. "That's an arm, that is! Now 'it me in the chest. 'Ard! … No, real 'ard. I won't 'urt you."

I put my back into it, and he never moved.

"An' all runnin' to seed," he said. " 'Now showin'! Now showin'!' No bellows to mend there, guv'nor. Teeth all present, an' correct, too, an' never 'ad a day's illness for ten years … But look 'ere! What I want to know off of you is this.

"Those johnnies at the War Office. D'you reckon they turns up the books? You see, Kitch, 'e says able-bodied men between nineteen and thirty, and old soldiers up to forty-two. And you say I look forty. And—see what I mean? If I 'ad a clean shave, an' sort of lost my memory for dates—what d'you think?"

"But are you really an old soldier?" I asked.

Mr. Butcher went to a cupboard and brought forth a waistcoat on which were sewn two frayed ribbons.

"China and South Africa," he said. "Discharged. Time-expired. What d'you think?"

"And Mrs. Butcher?" I asked, for the little room was very neat and tidy.

"Thank 'eving I ain't never loaded myself up with no womenfolk," said the veteran. "They 'amper a man. No, there ain't nobody to take no 'urt if— What d'you think?"

Last Tuesday I watched some three hundred of them going off for the final polish. They came along the platform with all the old swagger, with the steady, easy swing of good, trained men. Already they jumped to their orders with a click, and at the "Easy!" they sang like boys.

As the train moved away, one leaned from a window and called to me, a big, clean shaven man with frank laughing eyes.

"Cheero!" he yelled. " 'Now showin', now showin'!' But *this* ain't going to be no continuous performance."

The Decision

Facing the cool serenity of the lake, and framed in a background of glowing phlox and heliotrope, stands The Bench Where They Make Up Their Minds.

To look at it is just like all the other benches in the Park; and you must sit there to discover the difference.

Early in the morning the waverers come there in threes and fours, and talk with their heads close together; young men in corduroys, with luxuriant forelocks; big men with the knee straps that mark the navvy; youths with the office pallor on them, gnawing their nails. And some talk loudly of what they will do, and some sit and stare at the diving waterfowl, or seek advice in the lining of their hat.

Then they talk together again, and at last, squaring their shoulders, walk firmly and in step across the Horse Guards Parade, through the arch to Scotland Yard.

Yesterday morning one of the earliest arrivals was a neatly dressed young man with a tiny wisp of a moustache. He sat for some time fiddling with a big safety pin, a thing with a brass heart on it, such as grocers use to fasten their aprons.

He looked at the white tents that shone through the trees, at the clock, at a uniformed soldier who hurried past. Then got up and walked away from it all towards the peaceful blue mist of the lake.

A long while he gazed at it, his foot tap-tapping the path nervously. Somewhere in the silence a bugle rang out, and the man went back to the seat.

There was another youth there now, a short, thickset young man, well built and ruddy of face.

"Hullo, you!" he said to the grocer. "What you doing up here? Got the sack?"

"No—yes—at least, I don't know," said the other. "Just having a look round, you know. Slack, we are. Nothing doing, so I—I thought I'd come and have a look at the Park. What are you doing up here?"

"Me?" said the short youth. "Oh, I'm goin' to enlist."

"Going to enlist, eh?" said the man with the safety pin. "Well, look here, I—I rather thought—you know—I've been wondering how long it'd last. If I had any idea—see what I mean?"

"Longer we put it off, the longer it'll last," said the newcomer. "I reckon to get my Christmas dinner in 'Ammersmith all right though. And they won't miss me 'ere. There's mor'n enough butchers to go round. Gives me the pip, doin' nothin' but choppin' up joints when our chaps is likely bein' chopped up theirselves. They're doin' their whack all right. So I've come up 'ere."

"But you won't get your Christmas dinner in Hammersmith," said the grocer. "It's for three years or until the war's over. Three years, mind."

"Ah, that's only swank," said the butcher. "My boss took 'is shop on a ninety-nine years' lease, but 'e ain't goin' to live in it no ninety-nine years. 'E's fifty-four now. See? And talkin' about Christmas dinners, if some of us don't go there won't be no Christmas dinners for nobody. No turkey, no pudden, no nothink! See?"

He picked up a pebble and tossed it into the lake, shattering the reflections.

The grocer buttoned and unbuttoned his coat furiously.

"Well, look here," he said. "I've been thinking about it, and—well, I came up here yesterday and went home again. You see, my people are all in Middlesborough, and—"

"I came up here yesterday, too," said the butcher, and grinned. "But I ain't comin' up tomorrer. As to relations, that's where I score. Saw a chap come up on Toosday. Mother on one arm, sister or gal on the other. Marched 'im right up to the tent an' kissed 'im, an' shoved 'im inside. In public, mind! Catch me!"

Minutes passed.

"Nine o'clock, old sport," said the butcher presently. "What about it? Comin'? Can't make up your mind, can you? Well, toss up for it. Go on. 'Eads you join, tails you don't."

The grocer took a penny from his ticket pocket, flicked it skywards, caught it, and slapped it into his palm.

"Heads it is!" he said. "I'm with you. Come on." He thrust the coin into his pocket.

As a matter of fact it was tails.

The Sergeant

The long raftered room where on Sundays the children gather to sing hymns now reverberates to the rattle and tramp of armed men on Mondays, Thursdays, and Saturdays; fifty of us dressed in as many varieties of tweed and serge.

From his post under the picture of the Infant Samuel, ex-Sergeant Grubb, swagger cane under arm, feet at an angle of forty-five, flings us about, marches and counter-marches us, forms us into fours and companies, doing his best to convert a disorderly rabble into a body of disciplined men.

China, Thibet, the North-West Frontier, and South Africa; that is his record; and he is still adding to it, making soldiers out of clerks and hosiers and artists and plumbers, working like ten men.

For a while his little mannerisms amused us immensely—the swagger of the man and his strange words of command. But we all swagger now, and we begin to see why every order ends with "hipe." You cannot shout words like "arms" and "ease" with the proper staccato jerk. Therefore, "Ser-lope—*hipe!*" bellows the sergeant, and "Stand-at—*hipe!*"

Witness his singular style of instruction during a typical drill— "The pivot man marks time steady, Number One, an' turns slowly in 'is own length. That's better … No, no, you! Right turn! Right! The right 'and is the one you writes with, the one you're a-scratchin' your 'ead with. Do try an' bear that in mind."

At the "Dismiss," the rifles rattle into the arms rack, and we rest ourselves, aching all over. Then it is we learn from the sergeant much wisdom that is not to be found in the books. Whisky, we are told, is admirable for tired feet, but the very dickens when applied internally.

Socks well soaped at heel and toe will prevent blisters on a long march, and the finest cure for thirst is a plumstone perseveringly sucked. Also, given a ten minutes' halt, it is unwise to take off your kit, or loosen button or belt. That only makes it the harder to start again.

He tells us, too, of war as he has seen it waged—of yelling Boxers who carry little brass bells on their swords; of Pathans who move like snakes, using knives that "go through a man like cuttin' soap"; of tight corners when the Maxim jammed and only the bayonet remained.

"And if any of you lads gets to the front, I looks to you to put in one for me. I've been readin' about them Germans an' the women an' kiddies, an' it makes me fair itch to be at 'em.

"The Frenchies? Oh, you'd get on with them all right. I've met 'em. Not on business exactly, but enough to know. They're all right, all but their lingo, an' that's paralysin'.

" 'Ow they can fight on it beats me. There ain't a respectable swear in the 'ole French dictionary. An' a soldier's got to be able to stiff a bit 'fore 'e's any good.

"Our Tommies gets in a tight place, an' what does they say? They says—well, you know what they says. But a Frenchie, 'e says things like 'Name of a name,' and 'Thousand blessin's' and 'Blue wind.' Silly, I call it. 'Owever, it don't seem to make no odds. They're doin' their bit, an' puttin' it all out, too. But their supply of—what-d'you-call-it?—pro-profanity, is what you might call limited. Wouldn't frighten a Sunday school treat.

"I remember one man in my company. We was bein' inspected by some brassbound bloke, an' we got the order to ground arms, an' 'e drops the butt of 'is rifle bang on to his right foot. Fourteen pounds of it, wallop! 'Course, 'e couldn't say a word, an' I see 'im goin' white an' pink an' green, like 'e'd bin poisoned.

"Well, 'e 'ad to stand like that for best part of an hour, an' then comes the march past, another 'alf hour. But 'e stuck it. 'E stuck it good an' proper, an' when we got back to barracks 'e fainted before 'e 'ad a chance to ease 'is mind.

"When we come to look 'e'd broke 'is big toenail all into little bits. Not that that would 'ave mattered. Soon grow another toenail. It was not bein' able to stiff what did 'im down. Drove it inwards like, an' made a clot of blood on the brain.

"Not that I 'old with swearin', mind," admonished the sergeant, "but there are times when it's 'andy. There's some as is too lavish with it, an' I believes in savin' it up till you really want it. You ain't 'eard me do no swearin'.

"But when I look at those silly old stumps, then I lets it rip. Them two fingers in somewheres in South Africa. I looked for 'em, but I never found 'em. An' 'cos of that they won't 'ave me. I dyed my 'air, an' put my 'ands be'ind my back respectful like, but they wouldn't 'ave me. The ole doctor didn't 'alf laugh.

"Still, I got plenty of pals out there … An' some I 'ear as won't come back no more. So if I can't 'ave a smack at them 'eathen sausages myself, I got them as'll do it for me, an' please the Lord I'll send some more … Fall in!"

The Tactician

Not having seen Pettifer for nearly a fortnight, I had given him up for enlisted. Then last Tuesday I met him in the stationer's shop.

"Found I'd run out of Germans," he said; "so I've bought some more. By the way, are you doing anything this evening? … Well, then, come round and help me out."

There in the cosy room where whist and cribbage had so pleasantly shortened the long evenings, was a great map pinned to the table, and studded with gay flags.

"Beats chess hollow," said Pettifer. "Frightfully interesting. By the way, do you know anything about maps?"

"Not much," I admitted, "except that they're beastly deceptive things."

"Ah, that's because you don't know how to read a map," said Pettifer. "But how do you mean they're deceptive?"

"Well, I've got an atlas at home," I answered. "A really good atlas, but it's full of lies. For instance, on my map Dorset is coloured pink. Now I've been to Dorset, and—"

Pettifer looked at me and smiled wanly. He's an awfully good chap.

"What I'm worrying about is Old Kluck," he said. "Old Kluck and the Crown Prince's crowd. I've got an idea that we can get them in the neck. You see, here's the Longwy Gap, and here's Verdun, and here's Thionville. Now, if we were to—"

"But what's that thing like a hairy caterpillar?" I asked.

Pettifer raised his eyebrows. "That's a range of mountains," he explained.

"But they don't look a bit like mountains," I protested. "They're like wire worms."

Pettifer walked round the table to Switzerland. "Here's Kluck's lot and here's those other blighters," he said, ignoring my fatuous comment.

"Now, there's very little doubt that Kluck, if he gets half a chance, will rush his army through here, and then—"

"That wriggly thing, where you've got your finger," I said; "what's that?"

"That's the Meuse," said Pettifer; then he put his hands in the Atlantic Ocean, and leaned across Europe towards me.

"Is this humour or ignorance?" he asked bitingly.

"Humour, Pettifer, humour," I answered. "I knew all along. I knew that caterpillar thing represented mountains; great big heaps of dirt and stuff. I was only trying to brighten the business."

"Well, all right," said Pettifer, a little mollified; "but next time you're going to be funny, you might give me the tip. It's confusing … Now, as I was saying, here's the Longwy Gap—"

"But where do you have your meals?" I asked.

"On the sideboard," said Pettifer. "—and here's What's-his-name. Now in my opinion—" He picked up a bunch of Germans and ran a regiment into his finger. I took advantage of the diversion.

"Pettifer," I said; "can you form fours? Can you about turn on the march without falling over your feet? Can you Slope-*hipe* or Shoulder-*hipe* or Stand-at-*hipe*? Can you right incline?"

Pettifer rubbed the bridge of his nose with a battalion of Huns.

"Why, no," he said.

"Then what are you fiddling about with maps and flags for?" I asked sternly. "Why not come with me on Tuesdays and Thursdays and be sworn at by a real drill-sergeant? The Lincoln Green Emergency Defence Corps. That's us! Useful, if not exactly ornamental."

"But, I say," protested Pettifer, "I say, you know, what an awful ass I should look, marching up and down and all that sort of thing. An awful chump!"

"You would," I agreed. "We all did. Awful asses. But now—you behold in me, Pettifer, one who can score an 'outer' twice out of a dozen at threepence for ten rounds, who knows how many clicks go to a yard of wind on the back sight, who knows all—or nearly all—or, at least, something about refraction. And it's no end of good for you. Will you come down and join?"

"At any rate, it's doing something," he said. "But, I say, you know, what awful chumps you must look."

"That's half the fun," I said.

"And do you drill in the open?" asked Pettifer.

"In the open," I said, "with all the little boys being rude, and the little girls singing 'Johnny, get your gun.' You can still play with your maps, you know."

He was wavering, and muttered again, "At least it's doing something."

"Then I'll call for you on Tuesday," I said. "Now tell me about Mr. Kluck."

"But I can't think how you ever came to join," said Pettifer.

"Oh, it was old Livingstone did that," I said. "He came round to my place one evening and found me messing about with a map and some flags, and he called me all sorts of things."

"I see," said Pettifer. "Tuesday night, then … Now, about Kluck." He stuck some banners into the Vosges.

"If I were General French—"

The Battle Song

Although the chances are you have never heard of him, yet, with us at Lincoln Green, Major Grundley, J.P., is a Personage and a Power. While he has not exactly bought the village, you feel when you pass him in the street that he owns you.

All games are stopped as he goes by, and I have seen him stride like an emperor right through the hopscotch hieroglyphics of a party of little girls, leaving muddy footprints on their "Pudding" and "Beef."

There are no marks of the soldier about him. His face is, for the most part, dark red, with purple patches; his white moustache droops to his chin like two long icicles, and his eyebrows stand out like snow covered eaves. Not a man you would ask round to dinner or bridge.

It is in his legal capacity perhaps that he most shines. Since he was appointed to the Commission of the Peace he has missed but two sittings of the Bench, and on each of these occasions he appeared in the body of the court as prosecutor.

You would not look for humour in Major Grundley; but it is there all right. Four years ago he made a joke.

Paddy Greenslade had drawn his pension, and was before the Bench on the usual charge.

"We will make an example of you this time," thundered the Major. "No more half-crown fines. You will be crowned." And he looked round the court.

" 'Crowned,' I said," he bellowed, and Paddy wrung his cap in an agony of apprehension.

"Crowned!" said the Major. "I mean you will be fined five shillings this time. A crown."

How the court roared. The clerk nearly burst asunder, and dropped his glasses into the inkpot. And since that memorable day many an offender has escaped a heavier fine that the Major might have a chance of repeating his first great success.

Last night I was talking to Mrs. Butcher, from whom we buy our tobacco and christening robes, our jam and paraffin, our cheese and postal orders, when the Major came in.

"Prrrrm!" he coughed. "Prrrrm! H-rrum!" and tapped the floor with his stick.

"You-ah sell music-ah, do you not?" he asked, when his efforts to cough me out of the shop had subsided.

"There's a song I want, then, or rather a friend of mine in-ah London has asked me to get it for him. A patriotic-ah song. I believe our troops-ah sang it when they went abroad. D'you know the one I mean?"

"A patriotic song," said Mrs. Butcher. "Well, sir, there's 'Rule, Brittania'—"

"Pot hooks and hangers!" (or something like that) said the Major.

"—and there's the 'Red, White, and Blue,' " went on Mrs. Butcher. "Tuppence a copy, sir. Or there's 'God Save the King' and the—er—the French one. Tuppence each, sir."

"No-no-no-no-no!" rapped out the Major. "None of those things. It's—I don't know what the beastly thing's called, but everybody's singing it."

"Do you mean 'Everybody's Doing It,' sir?" asked Mrs. Butcher.

"Pot hooks and hangers!" said the Major. "No, I don't! What the dickens—you know the thing our—our boys sang when they went to France. Something—something about it's a long something or other. Some-ah music hall song, I believe."

I knew, but if I'd told him he'd have given me a month.

"Oh, you mean 'Tipperary,' " said Mrs. Butcher.

The old man took the copy and turned the pages. Then he hummed a little.

"That's it," said the Major. "That's it.

Goodbye-ah, Piccadilly

Farewell, Leicester Square."

(Here Mrs. Butcher joined in.) "Yes, that's the one. They-ah sang it when they left England. I heard them. And they sang it in France.

It's a long, long way-ah to Tipperary …

And they sang it in the trenches, too.

"In the trenches, by gad. Let's see, how does it go again? Ah, yes!" He trumpeted behind a purple handkerchief, then leaned confidentially towards me.

"But it makes me want to howl, sir, confound it—it does. At my age! I heard them at the docks, singing it in the dark. And they sang it in France, fighting in the trenches; and they charged to it. And, by gad, sir, they'll sing it in Germany before we're much older. In Berlin! 'It's a long way to—' I must get my granddaughter to play it over for me. Um! Ah! Yes! Hrrmpph! Prrrmm!"

"Algernon"

The sergeant brought him down to the drill hall with the idea of impressing us; a thick-set, stocky youth of nineteen, his neck and left hand all swathed in bandages, and bringing with him a searching smell of iodoform.

"My son," said the sergeant, and stuck out his chest like a pouter pigeon. "My son, Willie. Five engagements and three wounds. Mons, Le Cateau, Bon-something-or-other and two more. He'll tell you all about it, if you like."

Willie sat on the edge of a chair and blushed furiously while we arranged ourselves round him. After twenty minutes he began to thaw.

" 'Taint nothing," he said. " 'Taint nothing to make a song about. We was just fightin' and I got knocked out first pop. Hadn't been in the trench half an hour when I copped it—biff. I thought I was dead, but I wasn't; and before the bearers come along I stopped two more. Wasn't nothing to make a song about."

"But what is it like, lying in the trenches being fired at?" asked a chartered accountant.

"Oh, all right," said Willie. "Feel a bit stiff when you get out. There was a chap on my right. Toffy Simmons, he'd cut his thumb hacking at some barbed wire, an' he wasn't half grousin' about what he'd do to the Germans when he got at 'em. Said he was frightened of getting' some dirt in it and having lockjaw.

"Another chap on the other side of me was humming all the time, 'Anyone Seen a German Band?'. You know the song. Ticking 'em off in between, too. 'Got that one,' he says. 'That's four to me.' Then he goes on humming again. Funny how you could hear him with all that row going on."

122

"But what about your own impressions?" asked an immaculate bank clerk.

Willie looked blankly at him. "Don't remember much about it," he said. "But there wasn't half a row going on. Once there was an old crow come flopping along in front of us, and all of a sudden it sort of busted and all went to feathers, like. I reckon something hit it. The only bird I saw out there, that old crow was.

"Just before I took the count one of our officers come along, and give us all some acid drops out of a paper bag. They was all right, too. If I get out again I'm going to take some with me.

"Funny thing about that officer. He was the one we called Algernon. Always wore a Piccadilly winder on parade. Proper old Lah-de-dah, he was, doncher know, what!

"When he saw me laid out in the bottom and Toffy Simmons pinching my ammunition, he says, 'Hallo, Grubb,' he says, 'where'd they get you?' And he has a look at me, and cuts my sleeve up with a penknife, and he says, 'I wonder who the Spurs is playing today?' he says. Just like that.

"Then he stood up, and was talking to the men about a wind getting up, and how they was to allow for it, when all of a sudden he sort of slid down on his knees quiet like.

" 'It's all right, men,' he says, and sat down in the mud near me. Then he pops his head up and grunts and says, 'I should try at 900 yards, I think. Light's very deceptive, what?' Just like that. He'd got one in the ribs, but he didn't let on. Started telling Toffy Simmons about a retriever pup he'd bought in Club-row.

"Three quid he said he gave for it. I should think they saw him coming. Proper old Algy, he was. Sat there holding his side like he'd got a stitch and talking about all sorts of things. Showed me where he got shot through the palm of his hand in South Africa. Said it was like having forty thousand funny bones smashed.

"Then he spotted old Bonk Taylor further up. He comes from Woolwich, Bonk does. So Algernon sings out to him:

" 'Play up, Arsenal. Bet you a shilling they don't get in the First Division, what?'

123

"Old Bonk didn't half grin. Soon after that the Poultice Wallopers came along. But they took me first, so I don't know how he got on.

"Proper old Algy, he was, him and his acid drops."

The Mother

Judging by his bowler hat the man in the corner must have been at least sixty; but he cracked and ate interminable monkey nuts with the zest of a boy of ten. His wife held the bag, a little cheery woman, grey, but sprightly, with a lot of nodding jet on her bonnet. She also ate monkey nuts, sparingly, because they made her cough. They said no word to each other, but just munched.

From my corner I fell to watching them, and the newspaper slipped from my knees.

"Done with that, mister?" asked the man. "Thank you!"

"Thank you, sir," said his wife. He read her one or two extracts between nuts, then folded the paper slowly.

"Not much doing," he said. "This war business, I mean. Nothing exciting. S'pose we shall hear all about it presently. Mustn't be hurried, you know. Take your time, and do the thing properly."

"Don't throw them shells all over the carriage," interrupted his wife. "Put 'em in your pocket till you get out." She kicked the scattered husks under the seat.

"Do the thing properly once an' for all," continued the man. "An' that's what we are a-doing, French and Joffer between 'em. Mopping 'em up, we are. Absolutely mopping 'em up. That's what my son says."

The woman hastily took an uncracked nut from her mouth. "Our son," she corrected.

"Been out there a month now," the man went on. "Heard from him two days ago. Not a scratch, an' in the thick of it, too … Look here, mother, no more of them nuts. Presently you'll get a chest on you an' have to sit up in bed half the night, barkin'."

He cracked himself another, and turned to me again.

"So, you see," he said, "I've got a sort of interest in things. Makes you wonder a bit, you know, having a boy out there."

He took a bundle of envelopes and papers from his pocket and, searching among them, handed me a little photograph, one of those known as "sticky-backs."

"That's my Bert," he said.

"That's our Bert," corrected his wife.

"Not a good photo, though," said the man. "Don't show him up properly. He's a strapping lad, if you like. Five foot 'leven an' a half in his socks. He'll make 'em hop."

"Ah, that he will," said the mother. Freed from the hampering monkey nuts, she became almost voluble.

"He always was a fighter," she added. "From a boy. And that hard on his clothes, you've no idea. But he could always look after himself, so I don't worry much. Not really worry, that is. You can't help but be anxious like, can you? And not to know where he is.

"Sometimes, in the night when I can't get to sleep, you know, I lay there and go hot and cold all over, thinking about him. But in the morning I feel all right again, because I don't believe anything *could* happen to young Bert."

"He'll be all right, don't you fear," said the father. "He knows how to take care of himself. Nothing won't happen to young Bert. He's a lad, he is, and one of the best."

"And only last week," went on the mother, "I turned out four of his old shirts and cut 'em down and altered 'em for some of those pore little Belgiums. Shimmies and little knickers and things. Pore little dears!" She took another nut and toyed with it. "Funny he don't write, though," she said a little anxiously. "Only two postcards since he went away."

"Expect he's too busy," said the man. "No time to catch the post. Them pillar boxes in the trenches ain't cleared very often, you know." He looked at her narrowly; then laughed and said: "I know what you'd like. You'd like to be out there with him, to see he got his vest aired and his clean clothes all correct on Sunday morning. That's what you'd like."

The woman coloured a little. "Well, and what of it?" she said. "You can't be too careful, and he always was such a one to get his feet wet, and he'd put on his clean things straight off the line if I'd let him."

"You let young Bert alone," said the man. "He's all right. Having the time of his life, I shouldn't wonder. Nothing won't happen to young Bert … Our station, mother … Right as ninepence, he is. Don't you worry yourself about young Bert."

But as she went out I thought she sniffed a little.

When they had gone I still seemed to see the frail little woman, stroking one thin hand with the other, looking at nothing. Then from the other end of the carriage came a high pitched, feminine voice.

"And after what Mr. Churchill said about our Navy, and the sea being safe and all that. I think it's a perfect scandal, don't you? Tenpence for a plaice no bigger than the palm of my hand!"

The Atrocity

This matter lies on my conscience a little; say, about as much as an income tax return or a secreted garden hose. Not a lot, that is. After all, I can't go round telling people not to be so embarrassingly generous. Not mine to prevent the doing of good deeds, to spend my days nipping acts of kindness in the bud. Moreover, I rather like it.

In the beginning of things there was a banana skin, lying juicy side uppermost in the High Street of one of our Northern suburbs. Next, a bicycle, British made; and astride it a ten-year-old niece. Then an exciting interval with a yell in it, and a Boy Scout bursting with first aid and the resuscitation of the apparently drowned.

The doctor called it a Colles' Fracture of the radius, put some firewood and stuff round it, and told the niece that she must not move her fingers until the third day. Whereupon she twiddled them derisively, and her father paid the bill.

A week ago the niece, still in splints, came to stop with me, her uncle; and if I can only keep her arm from healing for another fortnight I expect to be co-opted to the local Brotherhood, the "Good-by-Stealth" League, the Relief Fund Committee, and one or two goose clubs. A bank manager nodded to me yesterday.

The Vicar began it; a worthy and throaty gentleman. He was passing by on the other side when the bandages caught his eye. Straightaway his nipped across the road like a lamplighter, and bellowed in a fruity tenor:

"Hello! Why, what have we here? One of our little Belgian friends? Dear me! Hrum, hrum! Indeed! Poor child. Poor little one! Yes! Hrum! Well, well!"

He didn't really give me a chance to explain, and the niece was out for glory.

"Dear, dear!" he went on, and tugged at the buttons of his coat. "Dear, dear! Er—will you—er—*permittez-moi*—er—*voulez-vous*—no, no, that's French, of course. Well, well."

He gave the niece a shilling, and shook her heartily by the hand that was not shored up.

"Niece," I said when he had gone; "niece, this is jam. I can see money in this. Tomorrow we will walk slowly through the park, and if you speak a word I'll tell your father that you're well enough to go home."

It was not a very good day, however. Sympathetic glances we got by the score, whispered remarks, "Poor little dear!" "What a shame," and so on; but all we collected was a rose, a kiss (the niece got that), some chocolate, and a cry of *"Vive la République!"*

Understand that so far I have said no word at all on the subject. My policy has been a strict one of *suppressio veri*. But the parson seems to have been talking overmuch, and my reputation for philanthropy is soaring.

A borough councillor at the station came from behind his expensive morning paper one day to ask after my "little friend." Was there any chance of saving the limb? Murderous blackguards, sir, that's what they were. Culture, they called it, didn't they? Had I seen the last White Paper? Women and children! Mutilated! He'd give 'em culture! He'd mutilate 'em! Barbarians! But it was a debt we owed to Belgium, and while the British Empire—here he went in for some figurative flag waving, in the middle of which I left him in a cloud of Union Jacks.

Again yesterday afternoon we were met at the street corner by a vulgar little boy, who made a funnel of his hands and screamed:

"Albert! Albert! Here y'are. Here she is."

Albert and another came along at the double, and there was a heated argument.

"Betcher she is."

"Betcher she ain't."

"You don't know nuffink about it. She's a 'trocity, she is. 'Ad bofe 'er 'ands chopped off. Bofe of 'em, by them Germans."

"Git out of it. That ain't the Germans. That's the 'Uns!"

"Well! Ain't 'Uns Germans?"

" 'Course not, fat 'ead. Germans is Oolans. The 'Uns done that. Chopped off bofe 'er arms, they did. She's a 'trocity, she is. There'll be a row about 'er, you see if there ain't."

Later. This business is becoming a nuisance. There were five urchins at the gate when we came back, and they all said:

"There she is. That's her!"

And one added, "Coo, lummy!"

The niece, at first indignant at being thought a Belgian, has entered into the game with spirit. I think she practices looking mournful in front of the glass. She will have to go home.

And yet it has its compensations. There is the bank manager who nods to me, and last night a beautiful lady called to leave a beautiful bunch of grapes.

"Pour le—no—*la petite*—" she began, then stopped. I suppose she had forgotten the French for "atrocity."

Discipline

In the piping times of peace Albert Grubb is a servile person who will carry a heavy trunk ever so far for twopence. He wears green trousers and a red tie, and is plain Grubb to most of us, and "Albert" to the man who minds the cab rank.

A mean spirited creature, we bullied him because the 8.15 "up" was punctual, or because it was late, and threatened to report him whenever there was a fog at New Cross; and he never said a word. Just touched his hat like a crossing sweeper.

But all this time Mr. Grubb was a member of the National Reserve, and owned a uniform and a waistcoat with the South African ribbon on it.

On Mondays, Wednesdays, and Fridays he puts on this uniform, and a lot of side; squares his shoulders, and straightaway becomes Sergeant Grubb, with the power of life and death over two hundred prosperous and well fed men, most of them fat and scant of breath.

For six glorious hours a week he grinds us beneath his heels, bullies us, and racks us until our joints creak, forgetting entirely that respect which is due to season ticket holders, some of them first class.

"Do try and stand up without leaning against one another," he pleads. "Dress by the right! Number! Form fours! Has that rear rank man took root? Now let me hear three smart clicks an' no shuffling. Form—fours! ... Rotten!"

At intervals in the drill he stops short, rolls his eyeballs upwards, and recites rapidly the names of the stations on the up line. Anyway, it sounds like that. Also he asks us "Did we ever?" and "Would we believe it?"

"You, in the white waistcoat." (This is a chartered accountant.) "Don't you know that seven is an odd number? Well, you can take it from me, two's into seven won't go. Now then, once more … You over there, if you've got what's-his-name of the spine I take it all back. If not, try and stand up as if you meant it. Feet at an angle of forty-five, middle finger resting lightly on the seam of the trousers."

"Sorry," the doctor called out, "but I thought I heard a button go."

"No talking in the ranks," yelled the sergeant.

From somewhere at the back came a shrill cry: "Nine Elms, Sevenoaks, Three Bridges, and all stations to the Helephant. Helephant train."

That, in the words of our instructor, "put the lid on it." He mounted a chair and drew a long breath. Heavily censored, his remarks came to this:

"Outside, you chaps may be bank clerks and doctors and lawyers, and all sorts of fancy things, and maybe you spend as much in a day as I earn in a week. But understand, while you're in here you're supposed to be soldiers, a sort of a kind of. And although I'm only the foreman porter, I'm your boss now, and I ain't taking no lip neither. No back answers. I've had some rough old lots to put through it in my time, but you—"

Of course the lower orders cannot be allowed to talk like that to the professions. So at the interval there was an indignation meeting, with the doctor in the chair. He was fine, and got awfully red about it.

"Shall we," he asked, "shall we, England's wooden walls, the last line, the forlorn hope, the bulwarks of Billericay, shall we—?"

And as one man the meeting said we should not. A parish councillor was writing to the War Office about it, or to the railway company, but his flowing periods were cut into by a thunderous, "Right markers," and we all fell in like lambs. Only two men fell over.

Once outside, the sergeant is reduced to the ranks, and becomes plain Grubb once more.

"By the way, Grubb," says the doctor, "I want you to come up tomorrow to trim the privet hedge and roll the lawn."

"Very good, sir. Thank you very much," says the humble foreman porter.

"And look here, Grubb," continues the doctor with a grin, "don't you think you might be a little more respectful inside there?"

"Sorry, sir," says Grubb, "but it can't be done, sir."

"I was hoping you'd say that," says the doctor. "And are we so very bad?"

"Putrid, sir!" answers Grubb. "With all due respect to you, sir, you're absolutely putrid! But I don't give up hopes of making something of you—in time, sir. Some of the gentlemen is so fat and slow, sir. But you'll be all right in time. If only we can hang this war out for another seven years, p'raps by then—"

To me, it doesn't seem worth it.

The Prodigal

This is to tell one Henry, late potman and marker at the Thistle, that his pal Jimmy is "in the pink" and "thumbs up."

The letter containing this information was brought to me by Mr. McKirk, father of Jimmy, and was dated from Northern France.

"I must deliver the lad's message," said Mr. McKirk, "but as I'm not much acquainted with public hooses, I came round to see you about it … Have your laugh out by all means, but I'm sorry I can't join ye."

The directory showed us four plain Thistles and five other heraldic inn signs, in which the national weed figured. I made a list of the addresses for Mr. McKirk, mapped out a route embracing them all, and gave it to him.

"It'll cost you threepence in tram fares, and say two shillings for extras, supposing Henry should be at the last one. Half a crown ought to cover it."

Mr. McKirk sat down heavily. "But, man!" he said. "Ye're no suggesting that I should call at all these—these drinking hooses. An' me a Rechabite for forty years! An' never set foot in a public hoose yet! It's no the half croon that's troubling me—much. It's the lad. To think that he's been visiting this place unknown to me! It's peetiful, that's what it is, just peetiful."

I told him not to fash himself, whatever that may be; and pointed out that in view of his careful upbringing, Jimmy probably went to the Thistle to play billiards.

"But nine public hooses in one evening!" said Mr. McKirk. "An' me never yet set foot in one. I couldna' do it. I just couldna'."

"Then now's your chance to begin," I said. "Think of the sensation at the Lodge. First hand information. 'Brother McKirk will now relate his horrible experiences.' Besides, you needn't drink. A ginger beer here and there, and maybe one or two small sodas. You must deliver your son's message."

"Aye, I must," sighed Mr. McKirk. "But ye'll come with me, will ye no? I couldna' go alone, I just couldna'. Nine in one evening. Man, it'll be awful."

We started out next evening, Mr. McKirk in a cloth cap, with his collar turned up by way of disguise. At the Cow and Thistle I pushed open the saloon door, but Mr. McKirk clutched my arm.

"Man," he whispered, "for any sake peep in first, an' tell me who's inside. Maybe there'll be friends of mine there, an' I cannot stop to explain, or we'll no get round the night. Peep in an' look if there's a man wi' red whiskers."

"All serene," I reported. "What's it to be?"

"I'll have a sup o' ginger beer," said Mr. McKirk, "but for any sake don't call me by my name. Call me Mister Broon, in a loud voice."

There was not and never had been a Henry at the Cow and Thistle, so we tried the Thistle and Leek, a mile away, with the same result. Here Mr. McKirk counted his money.

"But there's no need to drink at every place," I pointed out. "You can ask for the right time at the next, or change for a shilling, or say you've come to read the meter."

"If I must go into public hooses," said Mr. McKirk, "I'll no go in under false pretences. I'll drink." He did, too; ginger beer after ginger beer, until we came to our seventh venture, a plain "Thistle."

There my companion climbed on to a high stool at the bar as if he had been at it for years. "Twa ginger beers," he ordered, with the air of an abandoned toper, while I proceeded to question the pretty little barmaid.

Yes, she said, there had been a Henry there. Marker and potman, he was. But he'd enlisted soon after war broke out. A real good sort was Henry. No idea where he was now.

"I've a message for him from my son, Mr. James McKirk," said my companion.

"Never heard of him," said the girl. "Friend of Henry's, was he?"

Wiser in these matters than Mr. McKirk, I asked the young lady if she remembered Jimmy who used the billiard room.

"Jimmy?" she said. "Oh, I know! You mean Curly Jimmy, that went to the front. Rather pretty boy, with blue eyes."

Mr. McKirk groaned aloud. "Curly Jimmy," he repeated. "That would be him. And you knew him?"

"Rather!" said the girl. "I knitted him some socks. Rare old pals, we were. Had a free fight the night he went away because he wouldn't kiss me goodbye. Curly Jimmy! One of the best. What—what's—has anything happened to him?" She was fiddling with a silly little handkerchief.

"No!" thundered Mr. McKirk. "Nothing!" He fumbled with his boy's letter. "If you knew James," he said, "the message will do for you as well. My son writes—let me see—he writes that he is—er—in the—er—pink, and also that he is thumbs up. You, maybe, understand these expressions."

"Good old Curly!" said the girl. "Same again, sir?"

"Twa more ginger beers," ordered Mr. McKirk. "So you and James were friends? Then you'll maybe join us in a ginger beer? Thank you."

He climbed from the stool and took off his cap. "Here's to my son, James," he said.

"Here's to Jimmy and Henry," I added.

"Here's to dear old Curly and all of 'em, especially Curly," said the girl. "Bless him!"

"And didn't he really kiss you goodbye?" I asked.

"Ra—*ther!*" said the girl, and Mr. McKirk didn't even groan.

The Adventurers

A wisp of wind bent the tops of the three elms that mark the corner of Copp's Meadow, and a little shower of lemon-gold leaves fluttered sadly to the ground. Somewhere in the russet tangle of the hedgerow a robin sang, and across the cloud streaked blue a leisurely crow flapped homewards.

Near the cattle trod mud at the gate lay a derelict barrow, red with rust; and on it sat two young men. One, a youth with carefully parted hair and well chiselled features, bent over a blistered heel; while the other, a snub nosed boy with laughing eyes, lifted up his voice in song:

'Mid camp fires gleaming, 'mid shot an' shell,
I shall be dreaming of my own Blue Bell.

"Bet a bob I shan't, though, all the same. Wonder what you do think about when they're potting at you?"

The other said nothing, but stared across the field, where a rabbit sat up and listened. The songster paused.

"I couldn't 'alf do with a fine big beef pudden," he said presently. "All 'ot and steamin', with two vedge, and apple tart to foller. Not that I'm grousin' at the grub, mind, but my old aunt what I lived with, she couldn't 'alf make beef puddens. Nice thick gravy, too, and plenty of it.

"Look 'ere, old sport," the speaker went on. "You're a toff when you're at 'ome, I shouldn't wonder, and it's very nice of you to bring me out and buy me a beer. But talkin' as man to man, old pot, I 'ates the sight of you. I'm fed up. That's what's the matter with me. Fed up.

And I'd chuck it tomorrow if I didn't love you, and some other chap 'adn't got my job."

The second youth looked round sharply at his companion.

"Why, Jimmy, what's up?" he said.

"I am," said Jimmy. "Fed up, I am. Marchin' and formin' fours and right inclinin'. Presently we won't 'ave no feet left, and then we'll be discharged unfit. 'Battalion will advance,' and we doubles forty mile up'ill, and when we gets to the top, 'e waves 'is silly 'and round 'is silly 'ead, and we doubles down again. Then we lays in the mud and crawls a bit to rest our poor feet, and so on and so forth till 'Lights out.' "

"And very good for you, too!" said the other. "When you came up a month ago you couldn't run uphill without it was bellows-to-mend. Now you're fit as a fiddle."

"That's all right enough," said Jimmy, "but if they don't look lively this old war'll be over before I get a look in. I didn't join to go trainin' as a sprinter."

"I suppose not," said his companion. "But it's useful. And, by the way, why did you join?"

"Me?" said Jimmy. " 'Cos I was fed up. That's why. Six years in the same old shop, turnin' chair legs on a wood lathe. You put a bit o' wood in an' 'olds a chisel up against it, and there's your chair leg. Millions of chair legs I've churned out. Same time every mornin', same time every night. Same old picture palace on Sundays. Then start again at six Monday mornin'. I was fed up, I was. I wanted to see life."

"And you don't find this much different to chair legs?" asked the corporal.

"Oh, I don't know," said the other. "Its rotten, but it ain't so rotten … Look at them there rabbits 'oppin' about. Funny little beggars. Go all right with a bit o' boiled pork, they would … It ain't so rotten neither. But I didn't reckon on all this 'ere drill. I reckoned we'd go out to the front an' 'ave a scrap an' see life. I want to see the Frenchies an' the Russians an' them Indians—gherkins, don't they call 'em?—an' I want to see some of these 'Uns, an' 'ave a smack at 'em, too. Swines they are … 'Stead of which, 'Battalion will advance by the right … *Double!*' An' I chucked a cert thirty bob a week for that."

"You'll find it was worth it all right," said the other. "And you needn't tell anybody, but I chucked three hundred a year for the same reason."

The recruit opened his mouth slowly. "Three 'undred? What, quids? … Clarence, you're either a shockin' mug or else a beautiful liar. Three 'undred a year? Why, that's 'ow much? Six quid a week, Clarence. Come off of it."

"Fact," said Clarence. "I wanted to see life, too, so I volunteered for the front. I've never been to Germany, and this looked like a good chance for a cheap trip."

"Dyin' solemn?" queried Jimmy.

"Dyin' solemn!" answered the other.

"Then I take it all back," said Jimmy, "and I'll march in quarter column till I trip up over my whiskers. Three 'undred a year. I'm believin' you, Clarence, though it's a strain."

"And, of course, old chap," continued Clarence, "the sooner we're fit, the sooner we go out." He stooped to lace his boot, then limped up and down a little.

"I believe you, my boy," said Jimmy, "though there's 'eaps as wouldn't. And you and me, we'll go to Berlin together. First returns … It's four o'clock, mate, and we parade at 'alf past. 'In fours, by the right—' All the same, I couldn't 'alf do with one of my old aunt's puddens, and some sprouts and thick brown gravy."

The Deserter

Mr. Apps, senr. (of Apps and Sons, Jobbing Gardeners, by the hour, day or week. Quality! Civility! Punctuality!) gave up horticulture some years ago. The mower was too much for him; stooping, an impossibility. Success, as reflected in his waist measurement, hampered his movements, and he became a mere sleeping partner, chewing rafia, dozing in his potting shed, and making out the bills, while his son William earned the money.

Last Tuesday I found Mr. Apps, senr., breathless and purple, sitting on my dustbin, fanning himself with his hat. I asked him what was the matter, and he blew at me and rolled his eyes.

When he had recovered a little, "Silly liddle fule!" he said. "Wait till he comes back … Could ye give me a hand, mister, to hike her up the kerb? She be main heavy, and I so shart in the wind an' all." He slid heavily from his perch and led me to the road, where, standing in the gutter, was a great, big, fat garden roller, like Mr. Apps himself done in iron.

Together we got her up the kerb and down to the garden gate, where Mr. Apps sat down and felt himself all over.

"Something's bust," he said, "though I don't rightly know what. Could you obleege me with a piece of string?"

I went to find it.

"Or rope, maybe," he called after me.

"And now I'll just run her over your bit o' grass," he said, when he had lashed himself together. (That's how he talks about the Lawn.)

"But you can't roll the lawn with that thing," I remonstrated. "At your size of life, Mr. Apps, dragging siege guns about the garden might be fatal. And what's the matter with your son?"

"Blarmed little fule!" said Mr. Apps. "Right in the middle of the bulbses! And the autumn plantin' out! And the shrubses! And the manurin'! And the turfin'! Arl the year to do it in, an' her must go an' do it now.

" 'My king an' country needs me,' he says.

" 'And the bulbses an' chrysants. needs you,' I says."

Mr. Apps did one lap with the roller and sat down on the handle, wiping his brow with a piece of scarlet bunting.

" 'Lord Kitchener wants more men,' he says.

" 'And you wants more sense,' I says. 'What with wallflowers and polys. ordered for the vic'rage, and bone meal up at 33,' I says; 'and half a load o' turves down to the Nook,' I says, 'and fower ramblers for Muster Clark, and I dunna how many daffs and chewlips for the doctor,' I says, 'you ought to be thinking of other things than battle and murder and sudden death,' I says. Silly liddle fule!"

The siege gun did another half lap. Mr. Apps, no doubt, thought he was pulling the roller, but it was easy to see that really the roller was pushing Mr. Apps.

"And so he do be joined this here Kitchener's Army they do be tarking about. And I be a-doing the work and dragging this yer roller 'bout at my time o' life.

" 'Don't you worry,' he says, the silly liddle fule, 'I'll be back 'fore the daffs is died down to give a hand with the summer stuff.'

"All but had a row about it, we did. I told 'un he ought to have more consideration, and not leave me in the middle of the bulbses and the turfin', an' the manurin'.''

Mr. Apps wagged a forefinger like a sausage.

"And he ups an' tells me, his old father, as I be a fat old fule, that thought more of my business than I did of old England.

"Tidn't true," said Mr. Apps, as indignantly as if I had said it. "Tidn't true, and so I told 'un. 'An' if I was Lord Kitchener,' I says, 'I'd send you home again with a flea in your ear, so I would,' I says. 'You gert long-legged silly liddle fule,' I says. And all the rest o' the year to have done it in.

"Might as well have talked to this here roller. Didn't make no difference. Monday he ups and offs and joins.

"Not that I begrudge 'im if he's likely to be any use; and he always was a beggar for foigatin'. The money I've paid away for that boy! Winders broke and other boy's noses bleedin', and clothes all tore ... I did think a boy o' mine'd have more sense. The blarmed silly liddle fule."

I pointed out to Mr. Apps that in my opinion his son William had done the right sporting thing; that having no home ties—

"Home ties!" puffed Mr. Apps. "How about me? And I've got to drag yarnder roller all over the town. Home ties! And all these here tennis courts wanting patching up, and me got to stoop and stoop ... The silly liddle fule ... Not that I begrudged him, mind, but in the middle of the bulbses and chrysants.! It's crool hard, that's what it is, the silly liddle fule!"

The Xmas Egg

The Lambeth Guardians have decided that, in order that the Poor Law school children may have an opportunity of appreciating the position of national affairs, the usual practice of allowing each child an egg for breakfast on Christmas morning should be suspended this year.

The Guardian of the Poor sat taking his ease in his expensive drawing room. He had, to use a phrase of his own, "done himself rather well." A nice liver wing, with a piece of the breast, cauliflower with white sauce, crisp potatoes, something out of a bottle, apple tart and custard, and a taste of gorgonzola to finish up with.

His was an arduous life. From 10 a.m. to 3 p.m on Mondays and Thursdays he carefully guarded the poor as a good guardian should, striving to keep them from wine bibbing, gluttony, extravagance in dress, and slothful ease. His loud "Hear, hear," was ever at the service of the sick and needy, and many a starveling had benefited by his resolutions, passed nem. con.

Much labour of this sort had made him fat. His waistcoat from pocket to pocket was spanned by fifteen inches of gold chain, the pendant seal of which did not hang down, but just laid there, supported by the ridge.

The Guardian smiled sleepily and closed his eyes; then undid yet another button … The liver wing and the something out of the bottle were telling. The cosy fire helped, too. His several chins dropped as far as they could, and he slept a noisy sleep.

While he still rose and fell in the arms of Morpheus (and the god had all his work cut out), the door opened, the there came into the room a tiny little man, a shivering, puny forked radish of a man, and miserable blue nosed man with a threadbare head and rheumy eyes.

As he moved across the room a chill wind whistled through the house in the correct manner of the Christmas stories, and the clock on the mantelpiece (which was slow) struck five past nine with a melancholy sound. The Guardian sat up.

"I can see no one at this hower," he said. "Call at the offices of the Board tomorrow between ten and two. Shut the door as you go out."

"But I think you will see me," said the visitor. "I am the Spirit of Christmas Day in the Workhouse, and my name is Bumble." There were no fireworks; only that chill wind again that moaned in the chimney like a lost soul.

"I have come to thank you," the ghost went on. "To thank you for instilling into me new life and vigour. But for you I should have died a miserable death long ago, slain by peace and kindness and goodwill towards men." He blew frostily on his fingers.

"For some years now," he said, "things have gone hard with me. What with Old Age Pensions and Toy funds, and the growth of pernicious charities, my time had almost come. As it is I am but a shadow of my former self. Soft hearted guardians have hounded me up and down, decking even casual wards with barbarous holly and mistletoe, making life in our workhouses almost tolerable.

"That is why I so much appreciate your public spirited action in that little matter of the children's breakfast eggs. It was splendid, sir, splendid! Quite the old touch."

The Guardian bowed gracefully.

"A trifle, my dear sir," he said. "A mere trifle! Nothing to what I could do if I had a free hand.

"Here we have our Hempire fighting for its life; and pauper children keeping Christmas by gorging a new laid egg for breakfast. Stuffing themselves, my dear sir, living on the fat of the land, while our very existence is at stake.

"I asked the meeting, 'What do they know of Hengland,' I asked, 'who eat new laid eggs while Rome is burning, in a manner of speaking?' "

"A fine touch, that!" said the Spirit admiringly.

144

" 'Let them appreciate the rigours of the world war,' I said. 'Just as an object lesson, let them go without their breakfast egg, that they may understand the importance of the great task which we—' " (here he smote his gold Albert) " '—have undertaken on their behalf.' "

"And very right and proper, too," said the Spirit. "Quite like old times. I recognised you as one of the Old Guard, one of the *Landsturm* of Poor Law Guardians, a man of iron, with no silly modern sentiment about him."

The Guardian stroked some of his chins.

"Go on with the good work, brother. Go on with it! Down with their beer and tobacco! Down with their holly and mistletoe! Decorate the wards with oakum, if they must be decorated. Learn 'em! Learn 'em to be paupers! Especially the children.

"Why," he went on, "I've seen those kids in the ground of the— Institution, you call it nowadays, I believe—I've seen them dancing and playing games and skipping. Skipping, mind you! Paupers! I'd make 'em skip."

"Quite, quite!" said the Guardian. "The poor must be kept in their place. So I started on their breakfast egg. That'll make 'em appreciate the glories of our Hempire on which the sun never sets.

"I've got another good scheme, too," he went on. "Just to give 'em a really practical idea of what war is like, I'm going to move that on Christmas Eve they go to bed with no blankets and all the windows open. They'll know then what laying in the trenches is like. Or I might make 'em dig some real trenches in the grounds and half fill 'em with water. Or they might sleep in the open on Boxing Night; or …"

Other bright thoughts crowded into his fertile brain by the score; so many that under the strain he awoke as the clock (which was slow) struck five past ten.

The Historian

There is a fascination about watching other people work. You, perhaps, have stood in some busy thoroughfare gazing intently at the hot-footed Italians who sole and heel our asphalt highways. Or farther along, where a drain has failed in its duty, or a new tube is being punched into the earth, admiring the giant navvies who swing their sledges so unerringly to the chisel head. I was probably there beside you. Physical energy—other people's, that is—is a beautiful thing.

A morning or two since I heard the sound of a pick on the Horse Guards Parade, and turned to see three big men digging close to the archway. Being a ratepayer, I strolled across to get my money's worth.

Standing on a stone base was a great heap of tarpaulin, and round this the men were digging holes. I had never seen men digging holes on the Horse Guards Parade before, so I stood and watched, gloved hands snug in my pockets, pipe going well, while the three men laboured rhythmically, stopping only to wipe their brows with large red handkerchiefs. A beautiful sight.

As I watched and watched, there came a tiny voice at my elbow, a high pitched voice with a shiver in it.

"In the spring of 1848," it began, and then its owner came round, caught me by the second button, and fixed me with his glittering eye. He was a threadbare little man with a frayed beard, and he looked very cold.

"In the spring of 1848, when Haroun-al-Raschid conquered the Assyrians, the gun which is under that tarpaulin was captured by his men and presented to Sir Battersby-Tollemache. It is twenty feet long from breech to muzzle, and is ornamented with engravings of the life of Buddha. I've walked here from Clapham this morning, and I've had nothing to drink—I mean eat—since breakfast.

"In 1857 it was recaptured by the Montenegrins, who melted it down. Two years later it fell into the hands of the French once more at the siege of Seringapatam. Since I left Stockwell this morning I've had neither bite nor sup, and if you could manage—thank you very much, sir!

"This gun," he went on, "was cast by order of the Sultan Abdul Pasha, as a memento of his victory over the Turks. And in its manufacture twenty ounces of gold were used, and forty ounces of silver. In 1848 it was destroyed by the British at Alexandria, and yesterday I walked five miles after a job, and then didn't get it, being late owing to an ingrowing toenail."

My memory for details is bad, but that briefly is the history of the gun as told me by this interesting old man.

I paid for another cup of tea, and the historian took me by the third button, and fixed me with his other glittering eye.

"In 1848," he said, "it was recaptured by the British under Sir Battersby-Tollemache, and was melted down by order of the Government. From the barrel forty ounces of gold were extracted and twenty ounces of silver. The sides of the gun carriage, you will notice, are ornamented with scenes from the Arabian Nights, and I earnt half a crown last week addressing envelopes, but envelope addressing is not what it was before the war.

"But if you could help me to get to my married son's place at Leytonstone—thank you very much, sir. As I was saying, this gun was melted down by the French after the battle of Leytonstone." (I give you the gist of his remarks, although the facts may not be quite accurate.) "And in 1848, when Sir Reginald Tollemache—or was it Sir Reginald Battersby?—anyway, people came from far and near, and poured their gold and silver trinkets into the foundry.

"The beautiful engravings on the barrel, you will notice, portray scenes from the rise and fall of Sennacherib, but you've no idea how cold it is waiting about here on the off chance of a job. Since I left Catford this morning—"

"An interesting old gun," I said, as I paid out. "And when did you say it was melted down?"

"In 1848," said the man from Catford, returning to the second button. "It was after the fall of Khartoum. The French soldiers had heard of the precious metals used in its manufacture, and after a stiff fight they captured it. In the making of the breech 40lb. of gold were used and 20oz. of silver. Not that I'm begging, mind; but if you could manage it—"

It was an interesting story, and I managed it.

"And when was the gun brought here?" I asked.

"In 1848," he said. "The barrel, you will notice, contains 20oz. of gold and 40oz. of silver. A few years later, in 1848 I think it was, the French—"

"Halt!" I cried. "Never mind about the French. I want to know the history of this gun."

He fixed me with his glittering eye again.

"Oh, the gun!" he said, and I held out to him my second button. He took it and looked me straight in the face.

"In 1848," he began.

A Stocking Story

Robert Guthrie Anstruther was sitting on a pennyworth of chair in Broad Walk, swinging his legs and kicking the blacking off his shoes. He wore red socks and a white jersey and knickers, and his face was round and pink, and polished like the sunny side of an apple. He had a very bad temper, had Robert, and a very good nurse. Her name was Nanna, and she sat beside him reading "Faithful Only He: A Story of Love and Slaughter." So she did not notice the other little boy who came along.

He was a vulgar little boy, and his knickers were made ever so many years too soon for him, which caused them to be draughty.

On his face was quite a lot of Kensington Gardens, and he dragged behind him a wooden box full of dead leaves.

" 'Allo!" he called to Robert. "Come on, 'ave a game?"

Robert was astounded. "Dirty lil boy," he said severely; "go away!"

"Come on," said the other. "We're playin' wars, an' I've got a barrer full of dead Germans. Comin'? You can easy bunk away from 'er, an' I'll lend you my barrer if you ain't got no toys."

That made Robert wild if you like. "Dirty lil boy!" he yelled. "It isn't a barrow. It's a box, and it hasn't any wheels at all, and I've got thousands and millions of toys, so there, clever!" Then he put out his tongue, a thing which is *never* done by Kensington people.

That woke Nanna up. Captain Lionel, the rightful heir, had just come home to the Lady Imogen, full of honours and bullets, and Nanna was cross at being interrupted. So she carefully turned down the page, and gave Robert a good shaking.

"You'll go straight home for that," she said; whereupon Robert Guthrie Anstruther had a tantrum.

Tantrums are done like this. You take a long breath, clench your fists, stamp your feet, and shout "Won't! Won't! Won't! Won't! Won't!" till the long breath has all gone.

Robert did this, and before he could get his second wind Nanna picked him up, tucked him under her arm, and made for home.

The vulgar little boy grinned as he watched Robert's feet waving about, and said he was jolly glad he hadn't got no nurse.

That night, when Nanna went to tuck Robert in, she talked to him very seriously about the vulgar little boy. She told him of the thousands of poor kiddies whose only toys were sugar boxes and empty bottles and tin cans and clothes pegs; of little girls who had no fathers, and little boys whose dads were at that awful place called The Front. And she told him, too, about the Big "Star" Stocking that people were trying to fill with toys for the vulgar little boy in Broad Walk. She was, as I have said, a very good Nanna.

"And to show you are sorry," she said, "wouldn't you like to send some of your old toys to help?"

But Robert remembered that dirty little boy and the way he had grinned.

"Not thorry!" he yelled, and kicked the bedclothes off. I expect his liver was out of order. Anyway, he let the sun go down and the gas go out upon his wrath, which he had often been told never to do; and went to sleep like a cherub.

That night a pixie came into the nursery and woke Robert up with a wet sponge.

"I'm after coming to see if it's yourself that's sorry," he said, for he was an Irish pixie from County Mayo, and his father before him.

"Not thorry, not, not, not!" said Robert.

"Then I'm goin' to learn you," said the pixie (his mother was an Islington woman); and he waved his shillelagh three times in the air like a drum major, and said, "Gazeeka, gazeeka, gazoom!"

That did it! Things began to happen. Robert was in Broad Walk again, and there before him was a grubby little boy with draughty knickers, dragging a box full of dead leaves.

"Let me introduce ye," said the pixie. "The gentleman in the open work trousers is Master Robert Guthrie Anstruther, late of Kensington, now of Notting Dale ... Did I see a tear on your nose tip, the way you do be sorry for him?"

"Not thorry, not, not, not!" screamed Robert.

"And d'ye see yonder gossoon in the good clothes sitting on the chair with his tongue out? That's Master William Smith, late of Notting Dale, now of Kensington ... What about it? Are you after being sorry the noo?" (His granddad was a Scotch Water Kelpie.)

"Not, not, not!" yelled Robert. "I want my Nanna."

"Then it's after leaving ye I'll be," said the pixie, "and I wish ye a very good day."

You should have heard Robert. He had tantrum after tantrum, until they ran into one another. Then he got short of breath and just cried. Then he sobbed. Then he shook. Then he swallowed a big lump in his throat, and said, in a weak watery voice, "Thorry!"

"By the beard of me aunt," said the pixie, "but you are a one-er. I counted forty-seven while ye held your breath that last time. It's yerself ought to be a diver."

He then did some more tricks with his shillelagh, and they were back in the nursery again.

"Now, about those toys," said the pixie.

"Please, please take them," sobbed Robert, "and let me be Robert Gufrie Anstrufer for always and always, please."

And it was immediately so.

From the corner of the nursery came a rumbling and a rustling, a confused murmur of tiny voices; a "Who are you shoving of?" and a "Now then, clumsy," and a "Up you go, missis."

Robert looked and saw the lid of his Noah's Ark raised up, saw Mr. Noah climb out, and Mrs. Noah, and Shem, Ham, and Japhet, and two green trees. Then there came first the elephants, then the giraffes, the bisons, the goats (Billy and Nanny), the horses and cows, the dogs and cats, the mice and rats, the kangaroos and okapis, two by two (it was a ten shilling Ark), and formed a long line across the carpet.

Then a tiny bugle call, and a box of soldiers came open, and the little Tin Tommies fell out and fell in, with guns and bayonets and flags and horses; and formed up behind the animals.

"Battalion will advance, by the right. Forward!" sang out the pixie, and off they swung, Mr. Noah leading the way and playing "Tipperary" on the shofar, across the carpet, through the door, over the landing, down the stairs (you should have heard the elephants!), through the hall, through the letterbox, into the street, and so to the nearest Stocking shop, where they entrenched for the night.

And I think that's about all. Of course, the toys were all back in the nursery again by morning, because these beautiful stories are never really true. But Robert was sorry, which is the great thing; and gave Nanna heaps of his treasures for the Empty Stocking.

His sorrow lasted until exactly twenty past twelve by St. Mary Abbot's, when he had three consecutive tantrums outside the Tube because Nanna wouldn't let him play with the horse trough.

There is a moral to this story. It is, "Who gives twice gives double," or, in other words, "Girls and boys, share your joys, send along your Christmas toys."

One other thing: Captain Lionel, the rightful heir, got two Victoria Crosses, and was married, bullets and all, to the Lady Imogen in the last chapter; and Nanna shut the book with a sigh, saying, "What a frightful waste of good rice, and in wartime, too! Why, with a pint of milk and a new laid egg—"

The Unbidden Guests

The conductor laid down his bunch of tickets to help her, and there was also some outside assistance ("Now, then, mother, *up* you go!"). A strapping, bountifully made woman, with great bags of shopping threaded on her arms, and embowered in prickly green stuff, like Birnam Wood on the road to Dunsinane.

She came with a rush and laughed hugely; then turned to those who had propelled her, and expressed her willingness to do as much for them some day. One or two men were a little stamped on in her progress through the car, and the holly put in some good work. But she didn't mind, bless you! "Worse troubles at sea," she told one man, and left him groping among the dead tram tickets for his glasses.

Three vacant seats in the middle of the car provided anchorage, and she sank into them with a grunt, depositing her burdens about her feet and her neighbours.

Somehow she made a difference. The homeward bound tram is a gloomy vehicle these half-lit nights. A whispered conversation with a friend will make one the centre of interest, newcomers are frowned upon, and there is nothing to do but sit and stare at those opposite, who, like ourselves, are a depressing sight.

The woman with the holly changed all that. When she had got her breath in three great wheezy gulps, she took the chair and addressed the tram.

"Sprouts," she puffed, and everybody stared at her. "Sprouts! Three-ha'pence the pound, and I've been dropping 'em all the way from the 'Elephant.' This bag's got a leak. Heard 'em going pitter-patter behind me. You would have laughed. I could find my way back by them sprouts. Reminds you of the Babes in the Wood, don't it?"

No one said it did not, most of the company being absorbed in the advertisements on the roof. Not so the woman with the holly. She rippled all over with suppressed mirth, and shook like a jelly until the beads on her bonnet rattled.

"Nine pounds I started with," she said, between gusts of silent laughter. "Nine pounds. Three-ha'pence a pound. Pitter-patter they went. All the way from the 'Elephant.' You would have laughed. Reckon there's about a pound and a half left now. Pound and a half between nine of us!" She roared inwardly at the idea. "And all hearty eaters."

Next to her sat a lady, very upright and aloof, looking neither to the right hand nor to the left; two gloved fingers delicately poised on the handle of a tall umbrella held at arm's length.

"All 'earty eaters," repeated the woman with the holly. "Day off for me, Monday'll be, with nine to cook for."

She turned to her dignified neighbour. "Nice little family party," she said. "Nine of us, and all good trenchermen. You know what that means, I daresay, m'm."

The direct question could not well be avoided; the expensive hat turned slightly east, and the veil below twitched once.

"Thought you would," said the other woman. "Nine of us! I shall be up all night, I reckon. Puddings to boil and stuffing to make. And I must get some more sprouts, too." That started her trembling again, and she laughed until the berries fell off the holly.

The veil twitched again.

"Mine?" asked the woman of the sprouts. "Bless you heart, no, m'm! Mine! My word, if they was!" and another tempest shook her.

"Only five's mine," she went on when it had subsided. "Young Tom and his father and Milly and little Gracie and me. And quite enough, too."

The veil twitched in sympathy.

"You're right, m'm! But I don't mind. I didn't expect young Tom home this Christmas, and that makes a difference. You see, he's away in camp."

The veil sat up and began to take notice.

"Down at Aldershot. A fine lad, though I'm his mother. And that hearty! Believe me, m'm. I've seen him sit down to a beef steak pudding—but there, m'm, you know! A boy just getting his growth, and a soldier, too. They *can* eat when they give their minds to it.

"And he's bringing home four chums with him. Coming for three days, they are; four of them. Wrote me a postcard with not so much as a 'By Your Leave,' the young limb. 'Get some bren cheese in,' he says. I can see myself giving hungry soldier boys bren cheese on Christmas Day. Wait till I get hold of him. And sprouts three ha'pence the pound."

The veil had done a complete half turn by now, and was taking a real interest in these domesticities.

"I'll give 'em bren cheese. There's a turkey in that bag, m'm, that ought to do for five of us, and I'm going to get a bit of beef to eke it out. And there's apples and nuts in that bag, and that one's potatoes and more to come, and that's sprouts, what's left of 'em,"—she restrained herself nobly—"and that's—let's see—oh, yes, that's sausages and things to fill up with. Ton and a half altogether, I should think ... Bren cheese, indeed! I'll give 'em bren cheese, bless their hearts."

The veil asked a question.

"No, m'm, he says they haven't got any. There's one comes from Scotland and one's an Irish boy, I think; but they're all in the same regiment and nowhere to go to. So, as they're his chums, he's bringing them home with him. Like his sauce, too ... Bren cheese, indeed ... No, m'm, the Buffs."

The veil became animated.

"You don't say so!" said the woman with the holly, and her voice dropped. "Is he really? Well I never. That's funny. I'll ask my Tom if he knows him ... Oh, I see. And he won't be home? ... Haven't seen him since August? My dear, my dear! ... And not knowing from one minute to another ... Now hark at me rattling on. Of course, he'll be all right. You must make up your mind to that. I try not to think about it. We've got to keep smiling, and give 'em one real Christmas, them that can have it.

"I'll feed 'em up. I'll give 'em such a time as they never had before, poor dears … But you've heard from him, haven't you? … Ah, I was going to say! Every week. That's nice, isn't it? Makes him nearer like, bless him, begging your pardon, m'm …"

They got out together, the veil carrying the bag of potatoes, and you should have heard the sprouts pitter-pattering.

"It's a poor heart that never rejoices," said the big woman; then to the conductor, "Let me down gently, young man, there's a dear, and do be careful with the vittles. Come along, my dear."

Checklist of Issue Dates

The checklist below provides the original publication date in *The Star* for each of the sketches included in this collection.

"The Return," January 3, 1914.

"The Pedlar," January 17, 1914.

"The Piper," January 31, 1914.

"The Rising Sap," February 7, 1914.

"The Collector," March 21, 1914.

" 'Effects'," April 4, 1914.

"The Nursemaid," April 11, 1914.

"Wrigglesworth," April 18, 1914.

"The Goldfish," April 25, 1914.

"The Stores," May 2, 1914.

"The Gypsy," May 9, 1914.

"The Nightingale," May 16, 1914.

"The Excursion," May 23, 1914.

"Blackmail," May 30, 1914.

"Travel Talk," June 6, 1914.

"Garden Magic," June 20, 1914.

"Under the Tape," June 27, 1914.

"The Wise Woman," July 4, 1914.

"Two on a Tour," July 11, 1914.

"A Presentation," July 18, 1914.

"A Pathetic Pen," July 25, 1914.

"The Arrival," August 1, 1914.

"Called Up," August 15, 1914.

"Time-Expired," August 21, 1914.

"The Decision," September 4, 1914.

"The Sergeant," September 11, 1914.

"The Tactician," September 19, 1914.

"The Battle Song," September 25, 1914.

" 'Algernon'," October 2, 1914.

"The Mother," October 9, 1914.

"The Atrocity," October 16, 1914.

"Discipline," October 23, 1914.

"The Prodigal," October 30, 1914.

"The Adventurers," November 7, 1914.

"The Deserter," November 14, 1914.

"The Xmas Egg," November 20, 1914.

"The Historian," November 27, 1914.

"A Stocking Story," December 3, 1914.

"The Unbidden Guests," December 26, 1914.

F. W. Thomas

An Appreciation

The first article by F. W. Thomas was published on October 28, 1905. "On Getting the Sack" was sold to the *Morning Leader*, a Liberal halfpenny daily founded in 1892 and published, along with the similarly radical *The Star*, from the newspaper's offices in Stonecutter Street, London, E.C.4. Other articles followed, and within a year Thomas had joined the editorial staff of the *Morning Leader*, working as a junior reporter under editor Ernest Parke, who was at the helm of both newspapers. In 1908 Thomas showed his editor a humorous sketch he had written, asking him what he thought of it. Although Parke deemed it unsuitable for publication, he recognised his gift for humour and encouraged him to keep at it. Notwithstanding this, Thomas' excellent sketches and articles continued to appear in the paper on a regular basis over the course of the next four years.

Thomas' fledgling journalistic career with the *Morning Leader* ended in 1912 when the title came under the ownership of the Cadbury family and was absorbed into the *Daily News* to form the new *Daily News and Leader*. The London evening newspaper *The Star*, the *Morning Leader*'s long-standing sister publication, was also purchased by the Cadbury family. In May of 1912 Thomas joined the staff of that paper in their new offices in Bouverie Street; his first article for *The Star* was printed on August 14 of the same year.

From the outset, Thomas was a frequent contributor to *The Star*, where he remained for over thirty years. During this time he wrote hundreds of humorous stories and sketches and a regular Monday column that was usually accompanied by the artwork of numerous *Star* illustrators.

Thomas' most famous collaboration in this vein was with the noted political cartoonist David Low. Their successful partnership resulted in the popular "Low and I" series which began in 1922 and lasted for five years. The many humorous articles they produced consisted of reports of their visits to a variety of locations in and around London. These included such places as the Monument, the Tower of London, Billingsgate Market, the Serpentine, London Zoo, Madame Tussauds and Sotheby's. The "Low and I" series spawned two books: *Low and I: A Cooked Tour in London* (1923) and *The Low and I Holiday Book* (1925).

It could be said that the success of the series rather obscured the fact that the two had a slightly uneasy relationship. On arriving at Fleet Street all the way from Australia (he was originally from New Zealand), Low had expected to be working on a national daily. Considering himself a genius, he was said to have been somewhat disappointed at his placement on a London evening newspaper. With Thomas nine years his senior and, as the native Londoner, very much taking the lead as regards their location-based assignments, a little of the tension due to their different backgrounds and personalities does come across in the "Low and I" sketches. But the marriage of their talents produced some fantastic work, and over the years they built up a genuine fondness for one another. When one was off sick or on holiday, the other would "hold the fort" by carrying on the feature alone until their return. Thomas himself had some artistic ability and would enjoy supplying his own quirky cartoons in Low's absence.

This highly successful series finally ended in 1927, when Low left to work on the *Evening Standard*. After Low's departure Thomas continued the feature for a few more years, teaming up with the *Star* artist who signed his work as "Gee."

Down the years, Thomas' work for *The Star* also included a varied selection of informal essays and feature articles. Among these latter were a memorable series of travelogues in which Thomas documented extended visits he made to Paris, New York, Chicago and South America. It was on the first leg of this last trip, the background to which I will discuss in more detail later on in this essay, that Thomas met Rudyard Kipling in January 1927.

By chance Kipling was sailing out of Southampton on the same ship as Thomas, the R.M.S.P. *Andes*, bound for Buenos Aires. The night before embarkation Thomas had got wind of the fact that Kipling would be on board, and wired his editor, as any good newspaperman would feel obliged to do. After they had set sail the next day, the purser informed Thomas that he had made a faux pas, in that Kipling preferred the public not to know when he was off on his travels. Thomas apologised to Kipling and, in so doing, broke the ice, with the latter assuring him that he need not worry (as he couldn't have known), and besides, in his profession he was meant to be on the lookout for anything considered newsworthy. The two went on to enjoy a number of conversations on their way across the Atlantic. Years later these discussions formed the subject of a memoir that Thomas published in *The Star* in 1936.

Having published the reports Thomas sent back about his South American trip in 1927, ten years later *The Star* commissioned him to write a series of travelogues about his visit to the U.S.A. in 1937. Thomas' candid observations on the cities of New York and Chicago were well received, and were followed up by a string of equally funny articles detailing his visit to Paris in August of the same year.

But despite the importance of his travel articles and collaborative work, the bulk of Thomas' output for *The Star* was in the form of humorous writings which, for the most part, appeared on a weekly basis. The F. W. Thomas "Saturday Short Story" was a staple of the paper for decades, prompting the author and journalist Gerald Gould to describe him as "the man who is Saturday"!

Thomas was a gifted writer, equipped with a vivid imagination, an ear for dialogue and an ability to view commonplace situations in a highly individual way. This last aspect was summed up perfectly by a critic writing in the *Saturday Review* in 1923: "The most ordinary incidents furnish him with occasions of tenderness and cheerfulness. Mr. Thomas is a friendly philosopher—he comforts."

His stories were indeed marked by their gentle wit, lightness of touch and incisive insights into what makes people tick. These qualities were apparent in the stories he wrote about everyday London life, whether they were meditations on people's habits when travelling on the Underground, tales of put-upon City office workers, or the series of comedies which featured his outrageous fictional creation "Pamela," a scatter-brained high society girl.

And then there were all those strange tales set in a faerie world of his own devising that for years proved popular with readers of *The Star*. Peopled with an endearing cast of elfin folk and magical beings, Thomas' delicate, whimsical tales of fantasy proved beyond doubt his incredible versatility as a writer.

Perhaps Thomas' most important work for *The Star* were his many rural sketches, which he used in part as a showcase for his obvious love of nature and deep affinity with the English countryside. Several of these tales featured recurring characters, verbose eccentrics such as Mr. Grindle the Cobbler, his fatuous neighbour Simpson, and a small army of innkeepers, hawkers, shopping ladies and railway porters. Through characters such as these, Thomas (who after all was a trained journalist) used his powers of observation to good effect, employing wry humour to comment on the habits and foibles of people in rustic settings. He would also utilise made-up place names in his stories; the localities described therein would therefore represent just about any part of the British countryside. This aspect helped to establish the universal appeal of his humour. It is these latter stories and sketches, in which Thomas, in his own quirky way, documents his many hikes across the rural landscape, be it Sussex, Devon, or elsewhere, that comprise the main body of his vast literary output.

His writings for *The Star* and *Daily News* in this vein were well represented in book collections of his work. Hundreds of Thomas' pieces for the newspapers were reprinted in various hardbound editions. These include the best-selling volumes *Extra Turns* (1917), which was reprinted several times, *Saturday Nights* (1923), *Cobbler's Wax* (1925) and *Windfalls* (1932). All of his books were well received, and met with widespread critical acclaim, as reviews in numerous periodicals at the time testify.

Perhaps the most high profile critique of one of his books was by J. B. Priestley, whose esteem for Thomas was evident in a favourable review he wrote about the collection *Week-Ends* (1925). An ardent admirer of Thomas, Priestley reflected on the appeal of his humorous sketches: "The tales and sketches are the thing. They all have good ideas, of the kind O. Henry would have made into short stories, and, what is more important, they have a personal humorous flavour, that drollery which is unanalysable like a flavour or a scent, on the telling. The phonetic spelling itself is a triumph of observation." Priestley also felt that Thomas should be taken seriously as a writer: "Writing of this kind needs something more than a comic fancy, it needs a man who keeps his eyes and ears open and has observation and memory at the service of his calling. It needs, in short, a serious writer. That, I think, is the secret of Mr. Thomas' success as a humorous journalist. He is seriously occupied with the business of writing. He gives his work, however light it may be, however extravagant, the flavour of literature. He is, like all successful humorists, a sober craftsman and a serious man."

These sentiments were in fact an echo of some of Thomas' own thoughts on his approach to writing. In a rare interview printed in 1924 in his local paper the *Chiswick Times*, Thomas offered the following insight: "Let me tell you, being humorous is anything but funny; it is one of the most serious things in life. Anyone can be serious because life itself is serious, and it is no use to sit down and be tragic because, again, all things in life are tragic, but being humorous is the most tragic thing of the lot. You have to swallow all your own beliefs and opinions about life in general and take up an entirely new personality. People come to the office to see me sometimes and are disappointed. I believe they have expected to see a man with a red nose and a humorous cast of countenance—a sort of cross between Harry Lauder and George Robey—and instead of that have found a serious-looking young gentleman. It takes quite a serious man to be a humorist. As proof of that we have Dan Leno, whose great ambition in life was to play Romeo, Charlie Chaplin desired to play Hamlet, and my great ambition is to write a really serious novel, to do some good in the world. But humour has become such an integral part of my life now that I doubt if I could do it."

Beyond the readership of the *Daily News* and *The Star*, some of his sketches and stories found an even wider audience when they appeared in magazines such as *Lilliput*, *Tit-Bits*, *John O'London's Weekly* and *The Passing Show*. Thomas also co-wrote a stage musical called "His Girl," which ran for two months at the Gaiety Theatre at Aldwych in 1922. This extra exposure went some way towards increasing his fame. And who knows if his popularity would have expanded even further had he accepted the offer of Lord Beaverbrook (owner of the *Daily Express* and *Evening Standard*) to switch allegiances and come work on one of his newspapers for a higher salary? It's interesting to note that his old colleague on *The Star* David Low did just that thing, whereas Thomas is said to have enjoyed turning Beaverbrook down!

Towards the end of his long career with *The Star*, Thomas increasingly focused his creative energies on writing poetry. Prior to this, many of his articles and sketches had contained a liberal sprinkling of playful songs and verses. But throughout the late 1920s and into the 1930s he contributed to the paper a quite impressive string of narrative, story-length ballads. Some of these humorous verses were later collected in the book *The Ballads of Barnacle Bill and Other Jingles* (1943).

In 1929 Thomas found a fresh forum for his delightfully lopsided view of the world when he began a new column in *The Star* called "News From Nowhere." Renamed "This Cock-Eyed World" (later "Cock-Eyed Corner") in 1937, this was a mixed bag of jokes, riddles, musings and overheard conversations. It appeared in *The Star* on a daily basis, and lasted into the early years of the Second World War, when the column, at least in part, took on a satirical tone. On a visit to Germany in August 1938, Thomas had seen with his own eyes the persecution of the Jewish population by Hitler's regime. In the early months of 1940, Thomas used the final entries in the "Cock-Eyed Corner" series to poke fun at the Nazi propaganda regime. He was particularly scathing of Goebbels and the lies perpetrated by German radio broadcasts.

The ridicule Thomas meted out in this column and other articles with *Star* caricaturist Fred Joss, taken together with his prominent position as a long-serving journalist on *The Star* and *Daily News* (two newspapers that for years had been critical of Hitler's rise to power and the whole Nazi ideology), led to Thomas being placed on the Nazi death list, in common with his former colleague, David Low.

"Cock-Eyed Corner" was gradually phased out in favour of other features. There were for instance the brilliant "At Home with the Militia" sketches he produced in partnership with *Star* artist Leslie Grimes in the days leading up to the outbreak of war. In each of these pieces Thomas and Grimes would "fall in" with the new recruits at a number of army bases and send back reports of military life that were both illuminating and funny at the same time.

Following on from this series, Grimes would continue to contribute his regular "All My Own Work" feature, which showcased his fine cartoons and artwork in *The Star* for many years. A First World War veteran who had served as an air pilot and infantryman, Grimes also achieved renown for being the only British newspaper artist to visit the Royal Air Force in France in the weeks prior to the Allied retreat at Dunkirk. His exclusive drawings for *The Star* were flown home courtesy of the R.A.F.!

Thomas' work with Grimes made way for what proved to be a longer lasting collaboration with the legendary Roy Ullyett, another outstanding *Star* artist famous for his work as a sports cartoonist. The dozens of inspired articles they produced together were conceived very much in the style of "Low and I" and entertained readers into the early years of the war. The series was cut short when Ullyett received his call-up papers, going on to serve in the R.A.F. before returning to newspaper work on being demobbed.

The first few months of the Second World War were a particularly prolific period for Thomas, even by his standards. Starting in November 1939 Thomas compered the "Stories of the Home Front" column. In this feature he invited readers to send in anecdotes relating to their experiences of home-made trenches, black-outs and air-raids.

This feature proved to be short-lived, however, and was ultimately superseded by a column that Thomas had much experience of writing. In addition to his prolific output for *The Star*, Thomas had conducted the long-running "Merry-Go-Round" column in the *Daily News* (renamed the *News Chronicle* in 1930) throughout the 1920s and 1930s. Not dissimilar to the "This Cock-Eyed World" column, this feature was supplanted to *The Star* during the Blitz of 1940. A fun-packed miscellany of jokes, trivia, puzzles and readers' letters,

"Merry-Go-Round" sadly fell victim to wartime restrictions on paper usage. As *The Star* itself shrank in page count, Thomas' column got smaller and smaller, until by the end of 1941 it had been phased out completely.

Among his very last contributions to *The Star* were the wartime sketches he wrote as part of the "From the Coastal Zone" series, which ran from 1941 to 1945. These humorous pieces told the story of everyday life in a small community on the Sussex Coast during the Second World War. The locale was obviously Thomas' hometown of Seaford in East Sussex, though for reasons of national security the exact location was not revealed at the time. This aspect would have come naturally to Thomas, as he had for years been apt to use made-up place names in most of his sketches and stories. The "From the Coastal Zone" series is of some historical interest today, detailing as it does the effect on a quiet seaside town of the sudden invasion of barracked troops, gun emplacements, barbed wire, food rationing and German air-raids. These unique and fascinating pieces remain highly readable today, over sixty years since they were originally published.

Thomas' final article for *The Star* appeared in November 1945. In "A Word to Mr. Wells" Thomas urged readers not to take all of H. G. Wells' predictions too seriously, arguing that while some had turned out to be accurate, others had not. Apparently the general mood of the nation at the time this article was written was one of gloom, and it's perhaps fitting that Thomas signed off from *The Star* by telling everybody to "cheer up"!

After his retirement from newspaper work, Thomas collaborated with *The Star* and *News Chronicle* illustrator James Francis Horrabin by contributing songs and verses for his "Japhet and Happy" cartoon annuals (he had previously written stories based on Horrabin's "Dot and Carrie" cartoon strip). From 1947 onwards Thomas worked as a book reviewer for the magazine *John O'London's Weekly*. His contributions to this periodical, which lasted until early 1953, also included several feature articles and the occasional humorous short story.

A very private man, throughout his long career as a Fleet Street newspaper journalist he was never given to talking much about himself. Hard biographical information about Thomas was rather thin on the ground, indeed virtually non-existent are far as his many readers at the time were concerned. Even at the height of his popularity, reviewers of his book collections would note that about the man himself, little was known to the public. One could glean certain odd snippets of information from his writings, and make educated guesses about just *who* F. W. Thomas the man was. Readers could infer his literary tastes (such as his fondness for Shakespeare and Keats), that he smoked a pipe, owned a dog, was a keen ornithologist, enjoyed long walks, country pubs, good conversation and was an eternally patient observer of people.

As for the biographical facts that we now know today, our knowledge of his early life is limited to scarce items of information. It is known that Frederick William Thomas was born in Hackney, London on January 14, 1882. His father was a merchant seaman who later worked as a fishmonger. His parents had several children, and although he grew up alongside his siblings in the family home in Hackney, both his maternal and paternal ancestral roots were centred in the Rye and Udimore districts of East Sussex.

Thomas attended a Board School in Hackney but left at the relatively early age of thirteen. An avid reader who was largely self-educated and had a good head for figures, as a young man he obtained work as an invoice clerk for a commercial concern in the City of London. Finding himself unemployed in 1905, he began submitting candid articles about his jobless plight to the *Morning Leader*. The editor did not hesitate to publish Thomas' wry and honestly written contributions, and within a year he had joined the paper as a clerk. Soon afterwards he secured a placement on the editorial staff of the *Morning Leader*. Interviewed in 1924, Thomas recalled the background to his joining the paper: "At that time I knew nothing about journalism, except that you must write on one side of the paper only and not split infinitives."

Around the time he joined *The Star* in 1912, Thomas got married and moved to Chiswick in West London. For 17 years Thomas commuted to the City from this suburb, where he lived with his wife

Louisa Augusta (nee Podbury) and their two children Margaret and Peter. Meanwhile, his writing career went from strength to strength.

The aforementioned trip that he made to South America, which resulted in several articles, had a background of personal tragedy. Thomas' son died in 1926 at the age of 11, and in January 1927, the proprietors of *The Star* and *Daily News* sent Thomas on sabbatical leave, while he came to terms with the loss of his beloved son. A news item in *The Star* was published on January 29, 1927, informing Thomas' many fans of his absence. The following extract reveals how important to the paper he was: "The fact is that F. W. Thomas has been getting a little bit under the weather, though you would never have suspected from his *Star* articles that he was what is commonly called 'run down.' Thomas will carry with him the good wishes not only of his colleagues, but of the many thousands of *Star* readers for his complete restoration to good health—and high spirits."

Ever the professional, Thomas had evidently been working through his grief, and one can surmise today that his fellow newspapermen on *The Star* and *Daily News* could see that both physically and mentally he was running himself into the ground.

On the orders of his editors, in late January 1927 Thomas boarded the R.M.S.P. *Andes*, setting off from Southampton on a sea voyage that would last several weeks and whose ultimate destination was Buenos Aires. It was on the trip across the English Channel to Cherbourg, during which Thomas had the previously discussed meeting with Rudyard Kipling, that he began to compose reports on his travel experiences, to be posted back to *The Star* at the next port of call. Continuing to write his letters home as the ship made its way across the Atlantic to Pernanbuco and then on to Rio de Janeiro and Montevideo, Thomas' entertaining missives began to appear in *The Star* in March of that year. Published while he was still away under the heading "Chasing the Sun," the articles he sent back described his long train journey across land from Buenos Aires to Valparaiso in Chile, and from there his second sea voyage aboard the R.M.S.P. *Oropesa*. Stopping off at various ports on the coast of Peru, this second vessel eventually brought Thomas through the Panama Canal and across the

Caribbean Sea via Jamaica, Havana, and finally Bermuda before re-crossing the Atlantic and arriving at Plymouth in early April.

His odyssey to South America having taken over two months, Thomas returned to the pages of both papers in April 1927. In somewhat sporadic fashion, David Low had continued the "Low and I" column in his absence. Thomas wasted little time in teaming up again with his long-term colleague, while over at the *Daily News*, he resumed his weekly "Merry-Go-Round" feature, which Ashley Sterne had ably conducted while he was away. With his customary "Saturday Short Story" appearing every week, a revitalised Thomas was back on form in no time.

Two years later the pull of his family heritage proved too strong to resist, and in 1929 he and his wife relocated to East Sussex; a region where he spent the remainder of his days. Writing from his home on the South Downs, he regularly sent in his copy to the London offices of *The Star* and *Daily News*, occasionally dropping in to the Bouverie Street headquarters on visits to London.

Facts such as these, however, would not have been revealed to his readers at the time. What was known of Thomas as a journalist and humorist far outweighed the knowledge they would have had of his personal life, particularly in the final years of his career with *The Star*. To such an extent, in fact, that after his last piece appeared in a November 1945 issue of the paper, to the public at large, no more was heard of Thomas. True, if one happened to read *John O'London's Weekly*, or see his name on Horrabin's "Japhet and Happy" annuals, one would have been aware of his post-war output. But neither *The Star* nor the *News Chronicle* carried any announcements of his retirement and certainly no acknowledgement whatsoever that his long newspaper career had come to an end. Back then, his faithful readership on the paper would have been left wondering what had happened to him. It should be noted, though, that all this mystery was admittedly in keeping with the author's long-standing and carefully maintained privacy.

From my own point of view, having discovered his work so many years after he was famous, for a long time I pondered on the mystery of what had become of Thomas after 1945. This enigma lasted until very recently, when a genealogical researcher friend of mine managed to uncover various items of vital biographical information, such as his date of birth. And then, by coincidence, shortly after this I was contacted by Thomas' grandchildren, who acknowledged certain facts already guessed at and revealed much more relating to his life after 1945.

Thomas lived out much of his retirement at his home in the East Sussex seaside town of Seaford, where he had lived since 1929. After his wife died in 1961, he finally settled with his daughter's family in the village of Old Heathfield. During the remaining years of his life Thomas served as honorary treasurer of the Searchlight Cripples' Workshops in Newhaven, an organisation partly aimed at helping disabled war veterans. He remained an avid reader and enjoyed gardening, archaeology, wildlife and sitting in his greenhouse, thinking and dreaming away the hours. Thomas was immensely fond of his three grandchildren and was apt to entertain them with his poems, cartoons, and beautifully constructed models of villages, complete with ponds, churches, and hedges, etc.

Much loved by all of his family, he passed away at his home aged 84 on October 3, 1966. Among those who attended his funeral was Arthur Webb, an old colleague from *The Star*. Obituaries for Thomas were printed in *The Times* and his local paper the *Sussex Express*.

And so the biographical information and insights kindly supplied by Thomas' grandchildren now help to shape our understanding of his autumn years. With this newly acquired knowledge, one can only hope against hope that the day will come when more readers will discover the brilliant works of this talented writer. His legacy of varied writings is surely long overdue for a revival.

For now, I offer to the modern reader these new collections of his work, bringing F. W. Thomas' unique brand of humour and observational talents into the light once again.

Richard Simms
Surrey, England
February, 2010

Further Reading

The long career F. W. Thomas had with *The Star* is discussed in more depth in the essay "F. W. Thomas: Star Man," published on the internet at the following web address:

http://thestarfictionindex.atwebpages.com/f_w.htm

The same website also contains a comprehensive checklist of the short stories and fictional sketches Thomas contributed to *The Star* from 1912 through 1945.

www.ingramcontent.com/pod-product-compliance
Lightning Source LLC
Chambersburg PA
CBHW052134170626
46812CB00004B/1408